NIGHT TRAINS

NIGHT TRAINS

Peter Heath

NEW ENGLISH LIBRARY/TIMES MIRROR

First published in Great Britain in 1979 by New English Library
© 1979 by Peter Heath Fine

First NEL Paperback Edition August 1980

NEL Books are published by
New English Library Limited from
Barnard's Inn, Holborn,
London EC1N 2JR.
Made and printed in Great Britain by
Hunt Barnard Printing Ltd.,
Aylesbury, Bucks.

45004605 2

For Kathryn
who made this possible.

It is mind that deludes Mind,
For there is no other mind.
O Mind, do not let yourself
Be misled by mind.

Old Japanese poem

Quoted from: *Zen and Japanese Culture*, Daisetz
T. Suzuki, Princeton University Press, 1959, The
Bollingen Foundation Inc, New York.

Prologue

The Santa Fe boxcar had been on the move for more years than any man could remember; it was a steel box on wheels, a mute container of other things. Like the other 1,750,000 freight cars that circulated through the country it had drifted far and wide through time and change – a mote of dust blown by the laws of supply and demand: otherwise it was without meaning – except to the computers which stored its specifics in equally incomprehensible spaces. The only thing that differentiated it from all of the others was its cargo of the moment and that cargo's destination . . .

The sun had torched the earth for sixteen hours and then had left it to smolder in the superheated darkness of summer and the desert. But now a new star was born. The faintest pinpoint of light had appeared low on the horizon as if a spark had suddenly burst into flame, born out of cosmic events beyond imagining.

The spark danced on waves of turbulent air. It grew until it was a ball of light sweeping forward, thrusting space aside. The floor of the desert trembled and things scurried but were captured anyway, frozen in the oncoming glare that rushed forward down on the world.

Then, as suddenly as it had appeared, it was gone, leaving nothing but the steady click of the rails and the loom of box-cars passing swiftly in the void. Finally, even that had ended and there was nothing left but the red light on the caboose receding into nothing. The night train had passed. It was a commonplace and unextraordinary event, except that the train that moved this night carried the seed of death and destruction. Soon the seed would be watered by men of ignorance, men of pride, and men of anger. It would feed from confusion and grow on the ironies of circumstance until it was a monstrous thing: then like the genie in the bottle it would burst the very chain of events that had created it to become Fear, itself. That such a thing could happen was not accidental – it was inevitable. It wouldn't be the first time that Man had sniffed the consequences of his own actions only to find them too poisonous to breathe and yet too overpowering to escape. What traveled in the night had also been created by men. So had the boxcars, the train, the rails, and the computers which linked it all together.

All day long the freight and the Santa Fe boxcar had been moving across southern Wyoming, picking up and dropping off at depots, yards and sidings. Now it was riding light: seventy cars, the caboose and the two big diesels that had hauled them up from Cheyenne, through Laramie and across the Medicine Bow Mountains down into the Great Basin, Rock Springs and then the Green River where the water under the bridge footings stood in stagnating pools surrounded by vast middens of polished boulders, the gallstones of the Spring runoff.

The train idled through the outskirts of the town into the Yard. In the cab of the diesel men relaxed and leaned casually out of the side windows, to wave at the child who waved back and to catch a glimpse of a woman disappearing through the screen door of a paint-peeling house, summer brown legs and white thighs under the short cotton dress speaking of shade and honest, hard desire, the things that they all knew.

At the tail-end of the incoming freight two middle-aged security guards climbed stiffly down from the caboose. They ambled forward alongside the boxcars each carrying overnight bags. When they reached the center section of the freight they stopped momentarily and made a brief inspection of the seals on a Santa Fe boxcar. All was in order and they continued slowly toward the operations office through the ordered confusion of freight yard operations. Their names were George Sims and Marcus Whittaker.

Outside, yard workers and train crews mingled and stood in the shade of the boxcars. Switch engines were moving through the heat and dust and in the Operations Office teletypes began to clatter softly over the ever-present hum of the air conditioners. Beyond the yard and beyond the town there was nothing but waterless earth and empty sky.

Chapter One

The heat had seared the grass and then the earth, crisping it into lunar-like powder. The line of cottonwoods that half-circled the empty streambed had died years ago, but still they stood like Scythian warriors sacrificed over the tomb of a long-forgotten king, sun-blackened and twisted, pointing silent accusations at the terrible and aching empty blue sky. Beyond the dead cottonwoods and the dead stream nothing grew but sage. Nothing lived but lizards, toads and mice. Nothing moved but the sun. Over the streambed was the railroad trestle. Under it sat three men, waiting. One of them was a ranch hand on his way down to Reno, Nevada. Another was a wino already gone to seed. And the last one was Arkansas Slim who was heading for greener pastures by way of Salt Lake City. They were waiting for the freight to come through. It was 4:30 in the afternoon on the Wyoming plateau and the temperature was still close to 110°.

The ranch hand was a kid with a wind-reddened sad-eyed face who wore levis with enough dirt in them to walk away under their own power and a t-shirt imprinted with a giant set of human female lips all pursed-up like a cauliflower ready for kissing. The kid chewed tobacco and talked about nothing worth Slim's attention. Slim closed his eyes and let him ramble. The wino was already asleep. He lay on his back and snored. His fly was wide open and he stank to high heaven. There was nothing that Slim could do about that either except to move as far away as possible, and keep breathing slow and easy.

'What did you say this here place was?' asked the cowboy,

yawning and rubbing his eyes with the back of his hand.

'Used to call it Gollywobbler Flats,' said Slim. 'There used to be wild turkey here. Until they hunted them all out.'

'Don't look like nothing could live here to me. Nothing but nothing,' said the cowboy. He took aim and spat a stream of tobacco juice at a rock. Some of the spray hit the bum who didn't move, but started snoring. The bum's arm cradled an empty jug of muscatel as if it was his child, his only child in a world of the unloved, lonely and lost.

Slim remembered when the cottonwoods had been a pale, cool green, alive and the creek full of water tinkling down from the mountains. When the grasses grew high and deep and Indians lay hidden all painted-up and feathered waiting for the crunch of a bootstep, the sound of a voice. Waiting all the hours and days and years unspeaking, unmoving until the sun dissolved them into the dust leaving only the ghosts and the groans that he heard when the dry winds blew, when the moon came up and when his mind was roaming wonderfully through the shadows of his own imagination.

'First thing I'm going to do is get me a room and then I'm going to hit the town. I got 350 bucks in my pocket and that ain't hay. When that freight rolls through here I'm just hopping on and going straight to Reno, Nevada. I never been there before but I sure as shoot know where it is. You listening to me? You ought to be. Because that little old town ain't going to be the same when I get through with it.' The cowboy nodded his head and chewed his cud with renewed vigor. He asked Slim, 'How old are you, anyhow?'

Slim said, 'Old enough.'

The cowboy said, 'A room with a big, old air-conditioner, that's what I'm heading for – that and a piece of tail. And I don't intend on paying for none of that, neither. Soon as I get cleaned up they'll come running for it, you just wait and see.' The cowboy's innocent, young, blue eyes took in the sleeping wino. 'Whew – ' he said. 'I wonder where he's going?'

'He ain't going nowhere,' said Slim.

'Well he can't stay here. He'll cook to death. Well, won't he?' said the cowboy.

'Not likely,' said Slim.

'How do you know?' said the cowboy.

'He'll move along when he sleeps it off,' said Slim.

'What if he don't?'

'Then that's his business,' said Slim.

The cowboy kicked the rock that his spit had missed. He lay down on the hard ground and put his old stetson hat over his eyes. He was silent for at least thirty seconds. Then he said: 'Hell, I'm going to get him on that train. If he don't go somewhere – well, he *ought* to go somewhere because he can't stay here.'

Slim just closed his eyes and didn't say a thing. If he hadn't been tossed out of an empty boxcar in which he'd ridden into Granger, Colorado, by way of Boise, Idaho, he wouldn't have been here at all. But one of the yard-bulls had seen him climbing up inside and had tossed him out and told him he would kick his ass all the way to Chicago if he didn't get the hell off the railroad's property. There was always a few bad ones and some of them would even beat up an old man just for the hell of it, that was the way they were. So, he'd hiked up here to the trestle on the flats walking six or eight miles in the dark, knowing the way because he'd had to do it before in the summer of 1953 when the line was clogged up for a thousand miles with Army supplies heading for San Francisco and Korea. All that time had passed but nothing much had changed. The freights still had to slow down because the road bed was soft where the stream flooded out every spring and no one was going to do anything about it because it cost too much money then and now. That was it, thought Slim. No one was going to change anything and he couldn't blame them for that.

The dry wind stirred against his whiskers. He sat up remembering that he should get out his notebook and write it all down before it fled away and never got to be part of his life. He undid his rucksack, got out the spiral-bound pad and his ballpoint pen. He had left off writing three days ago somewhere up around Vancouver, B.C., sleeping on the beach until the mosquitoes got too bad. Then it was time to head south anyway, moving against the tides of humanity in their campers and their cars filling up the open space with noise, sweat and commotion . . . trampling down on everything just like the ocean, except this was a human sea.

The cowboy said, 'What the hell are you doing?'

'Nothing that you need to worry about,' said Slim, trying to think of the right signs for describing what it was like and how it felt to be lying on the beach with the ocean and the gulls and the stars and the mosquitoes too, all of it happening at once like being with a woman, meaning that everything was all wrapped up and inside out, at the same time and there was no knowing which was which.

'Them is pictures,' said the cowboy who had gotten up and was squatting behind Slim peering over his shoulder. 'Pictures,' he repeated. 'I thought you was writing something. Can't you write?'

'Sure I can write,' said Slim, 'and that's exactly what I'm doing.'

'What kind of writing is that? That ain't writing.'

'You wouldn't know. It's *hieroglyphics*,' said Slim.

Hero glyphics?'

'Egyptian.'

'Egyptian what?'

Slim closed his notebook. 'Hear that?' he said.

'I can't hear nothing,' said the cowboy, 'except the wind.'

'It's coming,' said Slim, strapping up his bedroll and hoisting up his sack.

'Well I don't hear nothing,' said the cowboy.

'Maybe your ears are too dirty,' said Slim.

'I can hear it now,' said the cowboy. 'Them old rails rattling. Come on and help me get him up.' He went over and shook the wino. 'Come on, you. We're putting you on that freight,' he said. 'It's for your own damned good.'

'Leave me alone and let me die,' said the wino.

'I ain't going to,' said the cowboy and grabbed him from under the shoulders. He looked for Slim but he was up by the tracks already. The cowboy was sixteen years old with a man's face, almost, and a man's body for certain. He could ride a horse and rope a cow but this was his first moral crisis – other than women, which was a different thing, altogether. The train was coming. Life was about to pass him by. He couldn't let it. He wanted it to rush him away downstream leaving all of his sorrows behind. 'Now, come on — ' he said to the wino. 'Shit — ' His hat was sitting wrong. He adjusted it carefully and started to scramble up the slope to the train tracks. Once you started out in life there was no going back. That was what his daddy had told him and he believed it.

When he reached the top of the embankment he dusted himself off carefully and took one last look back. The wino's eyes were open enough to see him and the wino's farewell was to slowly raise himself up, cast one baleful glance, and to offer the cowboy and the world in general a large finger. The ground shook, the dead cottonwoods rattled their skeleton fingers and the freight came through. When it was gone and silence again prevailed, there was a renewed outburst of drunken snores. The afternoon faded slowly away.

Not long before the day had entirely vanished the wino roused himself up and wandered off down the trail to town singing random songs of his own invention, as disinterested in the world as the world was disinterested in him. He didn't remember the freight train and he didn't remember the men who had jumped it. Like most of humanity memory had always served him ill. But forgetfulness had served him well; it had the sweet taste of pear wine and it came in a green bottle. He didn't know or care where other men were going because he knew for certain they would all reach the same place in the end.

It was 10:30pm. For two hours the freight cars had crawled through the bottom of a canyon under a sky that was alternately pitch black and then suddenly shattered by lightning strokes into a boiling cauldron of racing clouds. When the train left the canyon, the winds and the rain had come in a steady roar that drowned out all thought and all sense of being inside the boxcar where Arkansas Slim and the cowboy lay. Slim was used to it. The cowboy was afraid. Slim couldn't see him in the blackness but he could smell the fear and, now and then, when there was a lull in the hammering of the rain on the metal roof, hear the moans and the groans of an unhappy man. It was a bad one, that was for sure, but there wasn't anything to be done about it except to wait it out and, meanwhile, think of other things.

Slim was an adept at that. Right now, his mind was five thousand years away adrift in temples of gold and pyramids that rose from the beginning of the world instead of the end which was where History, that terrible phenomenon of time, had stuck him along with mass insanity in general and total confusion in particular. So, Slim lay in the dark at peace with himself and waited for the jerks and shudders and shrieks that would announce the perimeter of the Ogden Railroad Yard. When it came he was sound asleep. So was the cowboy: his yell woke both of them up.

'What in the hell's the matter with you?' said Slim.

'I was dreaming a bad dream,' said the cowboy.

'Well, you're awake now, and so is half of Utah,' said Slim.

'I thought we was going to Reno,' said the cowboy.

'Not me,' said Slim. He got up and cracked the door of the boxcar, peered into a cold drizzle, a fog-shrouded landscape smelling of salt flats and decay, of planetary sores festering on some forgotten limb of the universe. The freight moved slowly through a maze of signal lights across a wasteland of railroad equipment drawn ever-deeper toward the glowing center of all creation. Finally, it eased itself between two dark and silent lines of boxcars and stopped. It had come to the land of the Mormons on the edge of the Great Salt Sea bearing not gifts but misfortune from up out of the land of Caanan.

For Slim and the cowboy misfortune started with the sound of the footsteps on the gravel. Slim had heard the same sound many times before; sometimes it meant trouble; sometimes it didn't mean a thing. This time it was something worse, although he didn't know that until later. And, in fact, would never know very much more except that fate and circumstance had finally combined forces against him to prove that he was as trapped as any other man in the quicksand of events — this despite the fact that he had spent sixty-six years – give or take a few – moving fast enough to stay out of the way of the onrushing world.

The footsteps drew closer. It was two men and there was some talk going on between them about delays and telephone calls and San Diego. One of them said something about his bad back and the other one said, 'Let's go back up the other side, maybe it's over there.'

'No, it's right here,' said the first one. 'Santa Fe Number 3459. Put the light on it. That's the one.'

'That's the one, all right,' said the first voice.

'Well, let's get out of here,' said the second voice.

In the next split second something heavy struck something soft and then struck again. There were no voices anymore . . . only the groan of a man in sudden agony. Then there was a new set of voices but Slim couldn't make out what they said. This was because the sound of something being dragged across the gravel interfered and because the voices stopped as suddenly as they had begun. Then, not far down the line, he could hear boxcar doors being opened, then closed up again. Then he heard nothing more except the steady patter of the rain and the faraway sound of a yard engine rumbling closer and closer.

'I'm getting out now.' The cowboy's voice was all choked up. It was the first time he had ever been involved in this kind of trouble and his legs were telling him that it was time to run.

'Shut up and lie still,' said Slim.

'I can't. I'm getting out. I told you,' said the cowboy.

'You do like I tell you or they'll get you, too,' said Slim. 'Just hush up.'

'I'm scared to death,' said the cowboy in a plaintive little voice.

'Nothing to be afraid of. We'll be moving soon,' said Slim. Before he had a chance to add anything more they *were* moving and the cowboy kept his peace. For another twenty minutes their boxcar was shuffled around the Yard. The cowboy didn't know what was happening but Slim did. He knew Ogden like a bible. When the boxcar finally halted it was with a jarring crash against the coupling of another just ahead. The cowboy was all set to go again but Slim told him to stay put. 'You wait until I tell you unless you want to spend the night in jail,' he said.

'I don't want to do that. I'm heading for Reno,' said the cowboy. Confidence was creeping back into his young voice.

'Hear that, it's the diesel coming to hook up and get us out of here,' said Slim.

'To Reno,' said the cowboy.

'Salt Lake City and then straight through to Arizona. I'm going home to collect my social security,' said Slim.

The diesel hooked up and they were moving.

'I ain't interested in your social security. I'm going to Reno. What about that?' said the cowboy.

'I don't know about that,' said Slim.

'How am I going to get to Reno, Nevada?' asked the cowboy.

'Don't know,' said Slim, who knew perfectly well but had no intention of telling a young kid how to get himself in a lot of trouble for nothing except that he had to do what he had to do.

'Well, I'm getting out of here then,' said the cowboy. 'I ain't going to Salt Lake City. I'm finding me a bus.'

Before Slim could say or do anything, the kid pulled back the door and yelled, 'I sure do want to thank you, mister,' and jumped off the freight.

Damn fool, thought Slim. He got up and pulled the doors shut. It took almost more strength than he could muster, these last few months of traveling. Which was why he was heading where he knew he could have a good rest with his social security checks waiting, thanks to Homer Fergis, who had kindly bequeathed all his worldly possessions to Arkansas Slim before dying of pneumonia in a flophouse in Kansas City, Missouri, on a cold night in February eight years ago. They came in the mail just the same as if Homer was still alive. In a sense he was, thought Slim, settling back down on his blanket in the corner of the car. As he was dropping off to sleep, he had a quick vision of some yardbull seeing the unlocked empty and tossing him out. That wouldn't happen, he knew. This one was headed for home, back to the Atchisen, Topeka and Santa Fe Yards in Phoenix, Arizona. It had a home shop repair tag on it. By the immutable laws of Railroading it couldn't go anywhere else.

The convoy waited beside the empty platform. It had been waiting since dawn. The men who lounged in the shade of the four-wheel drive safari wagons and the high-sided transporter were sleepy, restless and bored. The Las Vegas Railroad Yard was utterly still in the noonday heat.

The freight coming in from Ogden could be smelled before it was seen. It rolled into the Las Vegas Yard under a scorching sun filling the air with the sickly-sweet stench of universal decay. A refrigerator car had lost its compressor. 80,000 pounds of beef had grown old quickly in the desert.

When the train stopped yard engines and men began to move. Swiftly, the delinquent meat car was towed into exile. Other boxcars were shuttled back and forth while some just stood. Fifteen minutes later it was all over. The yard was silent again.

Still, the convoy waited.

Finally, someone came: it was a man carrying a sheaf of waybills under his arm. He ambled down the line from the distant operations office. When he reached the platform where the convoy waited he asked who was in charge. A beefy-looking fellow wearing a sweat-stained company uniform jumped down. 'What's the story?' he asked.

'Looks like a foul-up,' said the Railroad man.

'What kind of foul-up?'

The man shrugged. 'Couldn't tell you that,' he said.

'Well, who's in charge around here?' asked the man in the company uniform. 'Where's my shipment and where the hell are the men who were supposed to be on this freight guarding it?'

'Wouldn't know anything about them,' said the Railroad man.

'Well, I'm asking you who does?'

'You better come on up to the office. Maybe they can help you sort this out,' said the Railroad man.

Together, the two of them walked up the track away from the convoy. Their figures danced and shimmered in the heat until they were twisted into the most bizarre of shapes. The sun beat down on the tracks and the long, silent lines of the boxcars which had come from a thousand different places to stand and wait until the time came to move again to a thousand new ones. The Railroad was a universe full of wanderers and strangers and, sometimes, the lost. Somewhere out in the desert was one of the lost. It was a Santa Fe boxcar. It carried a shipment of steel drums. Inside the steel drums was enough plutonium to burn up a city or two – enough plutonium to poison a few hundred thousand people – not enough to make an appreciable difference to the rest of the world. Not even the men of the convoy who had been employed to protect and safeguard society from such stuff seemed particularly interested. Two of them had dragged out old baseball gloves and were playing catch. The third was reading a *Playboy* magazine and the fourth was asleep. The time was 12:32pm.

Chapter Two

For Mulloy, the main attraction of the place was its easy accessibility. The Railroad ran right along the edge of what was left of the town. There was even an old station house long-abandoned except by an occasional bum and others such as himself who used it as a landmark to drop off the rear of slow-moving freights on their way up to the whorehouse at the other end of the street. The whorehouse had been there for a long long time and the train crews had used it well. Its offerings were as unpretentious as its clientele. Originally, it had been someone's house. Now it was just a pile of Victorian eccentricities where initial transactions between buyers and sellers took place downstairs under dim lights and mildewed curtains. Upstairs, was one room with mirrors and six without. Mulloy leaned against the bar and examined his dirty fingernails. He was a bull-necked bulky man with thinning red hair and a lumpy face. His eyes lurked behind formless slits of sunburned flesh: they were crafty, skeptical and shrewd eyes. He wore a highly wrinkled, green, dacron suit. The bagged trousers covered a shrapnel-riddled left leg and the coat covered the body of a forty-four-year-old man. For anyone interested enough to notice him, Mulloy looked like what he was: a Railroad security officer; a yard dick – a bull. Except for a couple of the new girls everyone here knew him already. He was a frequent visitor. It wasn't lust so much as loneliness, the kind of dull empty space that a man felt in himself when his life had little positive meaning.

Mulloy had been in Las Vegas for three days during

which he lived in a cheap hotel and spent most of his time lying on the bed, staring at nothing and drinking. He was waiting to be called as a material witness in the legal shenanigans called *The State versus McCready & McCready*. The latter was a law firm representing another law firm which had misrepresented the facts in a land deal involving some surplus property that the Railroad was trying to get rid of at a substantial profit to any fools who wanted fifty square miles of waterless badlands. Mulloy had been sent down from Ogden to bend the truth when called upon. No one had called upon him before the trial was declared a mistrial, and so here he was anchored to the bar of a house of ill repute with a few hours to kill until the next freight blew him north.

Pearl came down the stairs. Pearl owned the joint. Mulloy had come to see her. He knew it and she knew it. Neither of them could do anything about it. The thought depressed him. It probably had the same effect on her. She wandered around and talked to her girls and then came over. Behind the bar was a mirror and they both looked at each other through that.

'I got a toothache again,' she said.

'I told you, you ought to get it fixed,' he said.

'I'm going in on Monday,' she said.

'You ought to get it all taken care of,' he said.

'I used to have good teeth,' she said.

'Nothing lasts forever,' he said.

'Except us,' she said.

'Well – ' said Mulloy. 'I'll see you upstairs.'

He climbed the stairs and entered her own particular, private space. He stretched out on the bed and fell instantly asleep. Later on, she came and they did their acts of love and Mulloy fell asleep again in the hot room with the afternoon wind blowing the curtains and the sound of the trucks down on the highway rushing through the desert. When she woke him up it was nearly 4:30. 'They want you on the phone,' she said. His body was numb; his mind was in a fog. 'Come on, get up,' she said in a sullen, low voice, the one she used on the creeps when she wanted them out of her life.

He got up, put on his clothes and staggered down the stairs. It was his boss, Dietrich, in Ogden. 'What do you think your doing?' asked Dietrich and then answered his own question: 'I know what you're doing.'

'I told you I wouldn't be back till Thursday,' said Mulloy.

'Well, I want you back now,' said Dietrich. 'That means right away. Tonight.'

'Right away tonight,' said Mulloy.

'That's the message,' said Dietrich.

'How did you find me?' asked Mulloy.

'I know all your regular little stops,' said Dietrich.

'What's the problem?' asked Mulloy.

'You'll find out,' said Dietrich. He hung up.

Pearl was lying where he had left her. 'I got to go up to Ogden,' he said. 'Company business.'

She had a way of smiling that wasn't a smile. It was more like a grin of death. 'They didn't ask me, they told me,' said Mulloy. 'I'll come back down as soon as I can. We'll go into Vegas and have some fun. I'll take a week off and we'll get out of here. We'll go to San Francisco. What the hell, we'll go to Hawaii. How would you like to do that?' Mulloy looked at her lying on the bed. She and the bed were sagging a little. So was he.

'Why don't you buy yourself a new pair of pants,' she said.

'I mean it, Pearl. We'll get out of here,' he said.

'The trouble with you, Mulloy, is that you think you owe me something,' said Pearl.

'Maybe I do,' said Mulloy. 'I don't have time to get into it now.'

'Neither do I,' she said. 'Take care of yourself.'

'Sure, Pearl,' said Mulloy. He picked up his old leather valise and fled the premises. He walked down the main drag of the town, bought a six-pack of beer at the only grocery store and went to the deserted train station. When the six o'clock freight came along he jumped out on to the tracks and waved it down. He rode in the cab of the diesel to the next stop and then walked back to the caboose. He played poker with the train crew, drank his beer and slept the rest of the way into the Ogden Yard. Dietrich was there waiting for him surrounded by oak and wainscoting and sitting under green light from old Pullman car lamps. Dietrich was the Yard Superintendent.

Dietrich was a little porcupine crouched down in the middle of his nest. He was neither smart nor quick, but then they were all the same, the men in charge of things. Or so it seemed, thought Mulloy, not bothering to sit in the chair that wasn't offered. 'Now that you've told me that we've lost it you might as well tell me what it is so that I'll know what I'm supposed to find,' he said.

'Government stuff,' Dietrich muttered.

'You mean boots and jock straps?' said Mulloy.

'I don't find that funny.'

'OK, then it's something else.'

'A shipment from Hanford,' Dietrich said. 'That's all you need to know.'

'OK then, a secret shipment of boots and jock straps from Hanford, where they make them, and ship them to San Diego to be worn by the US Navy or, maybe, the Mexican Navy. I'll just start from there,' said Mulloy.

'You aren't supposed to know any of that.'

'Naturally. I'm just the tin-head around here. The security chief of this section. The yardbull. What everybody else knows I have to find out by asking asshole questions.'

'What do you mean – everybody?'

'Everybody,' Mulloy repeated. 'There ain't no secrets, my friend, worth keeping that get kept.'

'The goddamned Government,' Dietrich said. 'We never wanted it in the first place. That's a matter of record.'

'You scratch ours, we'll scratch yours,' said Mulloy.

Dietrich took a fresh cigar and chewed off the end and stuffed it into the corner of his mouth. 'You take charge of this, Mulloy. You do that and we'll make it good.'

'Sure. A gold watch.'

Dietrich stroked his chin. 'I'm going to tell you something.

A lot of people around here are getting sick and tired of you. And that includes me.'

'Too bad,' said Mulloy.

'Too bad for you.' He spun around in his antique swivel chair and looked out of his big plate glass window down at the Yard. 'Just find it, OK? Before they do. Before they get here, OK? We don't want them running around on our territory, now do we?'

'That's right.'

'Well, they'll be up here soon enough,' Dietrich said. 'And so will the Home Office. They'll be all over us and that won't help matters.'

'That's right.'

'The goddamned Government.'

'I'm going up to Operations now,' said Mulloy.

'They caught a kid last night.'

'Know anything?'

'They never know anything. We gave him to the Sheriff.'

'Tootle-oo,' said Mulloy.

'You report to me,' Dietrich said. 'Stick around here.'

Mulloy left him there, leaning back wreathed in a cloud of stink and worrying. It was good to see Dietrich worrying and with reason to worry, Mulloy thought. Someone was going to be had on this one. He could feel it already.

Mulloy went up to Operations and found one of the little grey men buried in among the machines and the print-outs and the telexes. 'We are now reconstructing last night's movement pattern,' he told Mulloy. 'Then it goes to Denver to be integrated with Western Area operations.' Denver was the capitol of computerdom. Logic Central. Where no mistakes could ever be made.

'That's very impressive,' said Mulloy.

'And then we have the other tapes. 'The ones they use right here in the Yard when they run them over the Hump. Everything that comes through here goes over the Hump and then we have the waybill numbers and the routing codes.'

'That's remarkable,' said Mulloy. 'Then you can tell me where the boxcar is that we're looking for.'

'Well, not exactly. It's a little more complicated than that.'
'It is?'

'Yes, indeed. In here we can only write the programs. Out there, things don't always follow the parameters indicated. I think you know what I mean.'

'Indeed,' said Mulloy.

'It is an extremely complex operation. You probably have no idea — '

'I was just wondering — ' said Mulloy.

'Yes?'

'About the programs.' They each cocked an eyebrow.

'Oh, yes. Done right here for movements in and out of the Yard – except for unit trains. Unit trains aren't broken up. They go through from point to point.'

'And who does the programs?' said Mulloy.

'The programmers, of course. We have about six of them.'

'Highly skilled professionals,' said Mulloy.

'Indeed,' replied the little gray man. 'We all are – up here, you know.'

'Sorry to take up your time,' said Mulloy.

'That's quite all right. If I can be of further assistance, let me know.'

Mulloy assured him that he would, and left him waist-deep in paper like an overwhelmed librarian sorting out the sins of the world which Mulloy headed for the land of the Saints.

The Sheriff of Morgan County had a fine new building to sit in and contemplate the Salt Flats stretching off toward the lake. But this time of night, the Sheriff himself, as would anyone who had any sense, was home in bed. A sleepy deputy took Mulloy up in the elevator to the detention wing and unlocked the door of the two-man cell himself and there was Billy B. Richards out of Empire, Montana.

The deputy shook him gently. 'There's a man here to talk to you. Come on, now, wake up.' He nodded and went away.

'Hello, Billy. How are you doing?' said Mulloy.

'Not so bad.'

'Never been in any trouble before?'

'No. I've been in lots of trouble. But ain't never been in jail before.'

'What kind of trouble? Want a cigarette?' He shook his head.

'Well, I banged up a car once. Didn't have no insurance.'

'And that's all, is it?'

'Until now, I guess.'

'Where were you headed?'

'Reno, Nevada. And I would have made it, too.'

'Never jump off in a Yard, Billy. What made you do that?'

'The old man said it was headed for Arizona.'

'Is that right?'

'And I got scared.'

'Is that right?'

'Them men out there,' he said.

'What were they doing?'

'I don't know what they were doing. Beating up on some-body. Some bums they caught, I guess. So when we started moving, I jumped.'

'And then they got you.'

'Not the same ones. Or I'd have been left for dead.'

'What about the old man?' asked Mulloy.

'Oh, him . . . he just stayed in there where he was. We'd been on that freight all the way down from Wyoming,' said Billy. 'He was a regular drifter. He told me to stay put when they opened up the car doors.'

'Which car doors?'

'The next one down, I guess.'

'And you don't know the car you were on?'

'Sure I do,' said Billy. 'It was going back to the Atchison, Topeka and Santa Fe yard. Had a repair tag on it.'

'You must be a regular drifter yourself,' said Mulloy.

'Not me. I just thought I'd give it a try. It was him that told me. He wrote it all down in a book. Picture-words. Said he was heading home to live on the Government.'

'Is that right?'

'That's right,' said Billy.

'Did he happen to tell you his name?'

'Slim. From Arkansas,' said Billy B. Richards. 'If you asked him a question he'd say it was none of your darn business.'

'That is interesting, isn't it?'

'I don't know,' said Billy, turning his flat, wide, high rawboned face down and looking at his socks which were very dirty and hanging down around his ankles.

'Well?' the Deputy said when he and Mulloy were downstairs.

'Let him loose in the morning. The Railroad won't bring charges. We'll have a bus ticket here for him. Get him on the bus to Montana.'

'He had $300 in his pocket.'

'Mail it back to him in Jerkwater. There a phone around here I can use?'

'Sure,' said the Deputy. 'Go right on in there.' Nothing made them happier than cutting down on the paperwork.

Driving back to the Yard Mulloy passed the local Temple. There it stood like an Egyptian tomb with the angel up on top with his trumpet, waiting to pronounce the end of the world, Judgment Day and the Resurrection – only the Faithful need apply. That rules out most of us, he thought.

The parking lot in the Yard was full of cars. Mulloy's office was in the old wooden barracks they had put up during the war. He wasn't there during the war – he was *in* the war. He called Dietrich.

'Where the hell have you been? I want you up here right away. There's a fellow who wants to talk to you from some damned energy and development agency. A Nip name: Shigata, or something . . . I don't know who the hell the SOB thinks he is but I want you to take care of him. He's on his way in from Salt Lake City,' said Dietrich.

'As soon as I can,' said Mulloy.

'I'm telling you, now,' said Dietrich.

'Just hold your water.'

'*Mulloy!*' he shouted.

But he had hung up. And then he had to run for the tail-end of the freight that was pulling out and heading South for Massacre Creek. He had a feeling – just a funny feeling that something was going on down there; that something was wrong with the methodological approach, not to mention the methodological minds. Having made this intuitive leap, he settled back on the lumpy seat cushions that someone had provided for the hard wooden seats of this caboose, and had a nip from his bottle of whiskey. People heard strange things in the night and jumped to all sorts of conclusions, he thought. If you took a scared hick kid's word for anything, you were in trouble. On the other hand, if you took the Company's word for anything, you were in trouble, too. Having reflected upon this, Mulloy took his second drink. His exercise in creative problem-solving ended and he floated away down the river of his unhappy memories. The freight train rattled and lurched through the night, making him feel like he was only the skeleton of himself. He took his third drink and while one part of his mind stayed on the river another part invented scenarios and motives. There were plenty of motives and lots of plot-action designed to embarrass people like himself. It was all a big game. The reality was out there. It was always different from what went on inside his head . . . or the heads of anyone else. He fell asleep knowing that something had eluded him, but not knowing how to name it or explain it.

What had eluded him would elude all of the others as well – until it was too late. And that was, simply that the irrational had its own shimmering logic.

Chapter Three

It was a place of desert, rock and dust. The man who stood on the rock had clear eyes, a powerful face and the voice of a prophet.

'Our Father who is in Heaven, hallowed be thy name. Thy Kingdom come, Thy will be done, on earth as it is in Heaven. Let us pray, in silence brothers and sisters,' said the man on the rock. He knelt down, his knees on the sharp lava that formed the outcropping which they used as the altar of God. The others followed and cast themselves down with the desert wind whispering, stirring a beard, blowing the long hair of the women. Fifteen people prostrated themselves in the hard, hot light.

When the hour of silence had passed, the leader rose up. His eyes moved from one to the next. 'Sister Martha,' he said. 'Do you have testimony?'

She raised herself. 'No,' she said but her eyes wandered away from his own. They were weak, blue and timid.

'Were you not sinful in your thoughts?' said the leader.

'No,' said Sister Martha.

'Speak these words to God,' he said. 'I was not sinful before you.'

'I was not sinful before You,' said Sister Martha.

'Now, speak them to me,' he said.

'I was sinful. I had thoughts,' said Sister Martha.

'Of what? Tell the Lord.'

'Of my child,' said Sister Martha.

'What thoughts?'

'That the Lord wanted him here, with me.'

'The Lord wants him where he is,' said the leader. 'The Lord put him there and that is the will of God.'

Sister Martha nodded then lowered her head.

'When the Lord took the children of Sister Rachel, he did not forsake her. When the Lord took the child of Sister Sarah, he did not forsake her. Just as when the Lord took the sons of Abraham, he did not forsake him.'

'Amen — ' said the people kneeling on the rocks.

'Thou shall love the Lord, his judgments and commandments,' said Simon.

'Amen — ' said the people kneeling on the rocks.

'Fear none of those things which thou shalt suffer,' he said.

'Amen — '

'He that overcomes shall sit on my throne.'

'Amen!'

'Fear Him and give glory to Him for the hour of His judgment is near,' he shouted. 'Redemption is in His hands!'

'*Amen!*' they all shouted and raised their hands to the sky.

'Now, let us return to our work,' said the leader. 'Martha, you stay here. The Lord will give you strength.' He turned and walked down the hill toward the camp. The others followed.

An hour later he left in an old pickup truck. He followed the tire tracks in the sand until he reached the dry river bottom. On the other side a dirt track wandered off toward the distant red cliffs of the Pancake mountains. Beyond that was the road that led to the highway which would take him to the Railroad siding at Copper Flat, the siding where his brother would be waiting. The siding where there was work to be done. The Lord's work. And he was ready. Ready to finish what had begun long ago – first in his heart and then in his mind, like fire burning through his soul, the ashes scattered on the winds leaving nothing but purity and purpose and will. As his father had been an instrument, he would be an instrument. As his father had fallen, he would not. As his father had handled the snake, he would hold

Satan in his own hand. As his father had held the snake and the snake had struck deep into the soul of his father, he would hold Satan but Satan would not strike. Not until so commanded by God, ruler of all things, keeper of souls, merciful and Almighty.

A pheasant in glorious plumage had burst from behind a rock. He drove over it without looking back. It lay crushed in the dust.

Chapter Four

When the call from Nevada came it was 4:15 in the afternoon at San Francisco's Fairmont Hotel. Under the beautiful chandeliers of the Sutter Room and in the shade of huge
potted palms, two hundred and fifty well-heeled Friends,
lovers, sons, daughters and more distant relatives of The
Earth had gathered to eat, drink and pay homage to clean
air, blue skies and Environmental Protection Agency
emission controls. They had also come, these handsome men
and women from the garden suburbs of Marin County, Mill
Valley, Big Sur, Northern California and Santa Barbara to
give polite attention to their enemy. He was Eddie Shigata,
one of the honored speakers, and the enmity was confined
to a polite tinkling of applause when he took the podium.
However, neither he nor they had any doubt that politically,
socially and philosophically they stood a hundred light years
apart . . . or maybe further on the question of nuclear power.

Eddie's little talk was brief. He knew his audience too well
to believe that anything he said would have much effect on
their position – or his. He described the benefits, weighed the
risks. No charts, gobbledygook or slick conundrums. Just
an honest and simple appraisal of the problems leading
swiftly to what they really wanted – the open question
period wherein all that was worthy – and a lot that wasn't –
would be scribbled down by the two yawning reporters sitting at the back of the banquet room to duly appear in
tomorrow's newspapers.

'Isn't it true —' began a tall, bronzed, middle-aged gentleman in a Harvard drawl that spoke of places that Eddie

would never know. 'Isn't it true that the regulatory agencies have a long history of shifting their policy in order to please certain congressmen with budgetary powers?' He then went on to answer his own question.

When he was finished Eddie said, 'I think that those abuses have been largely eliminated by the new Federal Guidelines. However, that doesn't mean that Government is infallible – or General Electric.'

The response got its titter. And the gentleman sat down.

A long-haired type with Sierra Club written all over him got up.

'Let's get into the risk quotient,' he said. 'Isn't it a fact that a reactor core melt down will contaminate hundreds, perhaps thousands of square miles with highly toxic radioactive waste and isn't it a fact that the Sandia Report states that the occasional failure of emergency cooling systems is highly probable in a full-scale nuclear economy and isn't it a fact that a major accident of this type would approximate the radiological effects of a twenty megaton hydrogen bomb dropped let's say on New York?'

'If such an accident were to occur,' said Eddie watching the pencils held by the Press fly, 'the effects are likely to be manifested on a much smaller scale.'

'Well, then, how about a Hiroshima size bomb? How about a nuclear accident equivalent in casualties to what they dropped on Japan?' the long-haired questioner scowled up at Eddie Shigata, traitor to his race.

A hush had fallen over the audience. Perhaps it was embarrasment at the intentional coupling of an inverted racism with issues that concerned all of humanity.

Eddie smiled wearily. 'I wasn't in Japan when they dropped the bomb,' he said. 'I was in a detention camp for Japanese Americans in Northern California. However — ' he started but a hand touched him on the shoulder and a man whispered. 'It's your office calling. They say it's urgent. I'll take over for a few minutes, if you like.'

He excused himself, threaded his way through the tables and took the call on a plug-in phone held by a bellboy. It was from the Materials Security and Transfer Section of the Nevada Operations Office, where he had started the day before taking the plane to San Francisco.

'Seems there's a little problem here,' said the man at the other end. Rosen, thought Eddie. A little guy in white shirt-sleeves who worked in Materials Accountancy. 'Seems one of the Hanford shipments got lost somewhere on its way down,' said Rosen. 'Seems there was a lot of flooding last night up north and they had to re-route a lot of traffic.

'You must have heard from the security team,' said Eddie.

'That's the funny thing,' said Rosen. 'Seems they never checked in after Ogden.'

'When was that?' asked Eddie.

'About seventeen hours ago,' said Rosen.

'Anybody doing anything?' said Eddie.

'Well, we didn't know about it until a couple of hours ago. Security Services were checking it out. They're ones that handle the shipments,' said Rosen. 'Guess they wanted to make sure.'

'Of what?'

'That it wasn't their fault,' said Rosen. 'You know how these contract outfits are.'

'Davis know about it?' Chet Davis was Chief of Operations, Region IV, The Environmental Research and Development Agency. Eddie was in charge of the Field Services Inspection Office. Davis was in Washington, DC for three days.

'Tried to reach him. He's checked out. Probably on the plane home,' said Rosen.

'OK,' said Eddie. 'See if you can reach him on the plane. If you can't, just sit tight. I'll be back as soon as I can get on a flight out of here.'

'Right on,' said Rosen.

'One other thing — ' said Eddie. 'Keep the lid on it. Tight.'

'You know it,' said Rosen.

And the last question, the one Eddie didn't really want to ask because he knew the answer. 'What was the shipment?'

'SNM,' said Rosen. 'Delta Phase. It was going into the West Valley Breeder project.'

'How much?' asked Eddie.

'Seems there was enough,' said Rosen.

'I don't care what it *seems*,' said Eddie. 'How much?'

'Forty-five kilograms,' said Rosen, in hurt tones. 'I was about to tell you.'

'I'm sorry,' said Eddie. 'It's been a hard day.'

'Sure,' said Rosen. 'I understand.'

'I'll be on the next plane,' said Eddie. 'And see if you can find out anything from the Railroad.'

He hung up and stood looking through a window down at the streamers of fog which were sweeping over the city like whipped cream spilling from an overturned bowl, or a mix-master gone wild. First the fog and then the night, he thought.

'Sir — ' It was the bellboy, who was old enough to be Eddie's father, who was dead. He wanted the telephone back. When Eddie gave it to him he unplugged it and carried it away cradled in his arms like a fancy poodle. From inside the Sutter Room there was a burst of applause. He took the elevator down to the lobby, wrote a brief note to the Chairman of the meeting, sent it upstairs, and took a taxi to the airport. Enough – his mind repeated. Enough for what? For anything – if one only knew. For nothing, if you didn't. The cab dove into the fog and they were lost in another world of dreams and subtleties. He would have to call Janet somewhere along the way. There wouldn't be time to stop by the house. Things would sort themselves out in a few hours. No need to think about cancelling any plans. They would be landing in Rome on Saturday with a month to spend with each other, the first month in a long time. The kids were going to Ojai to stay with Janet's parents. To be spoiled and over-attended in the world of the well-to-do *wasps* – her world, not his. *The Ranch*, they called it – her parents. The only thing it raised was golf balls and flower arrangements. His own mother lived with an aunt in West Los Angeles, the old capital of Niseidom, in a little frame house surrounded by dreary apartment buildings. His mother was a little old Japanese lady with a wizened face who had never seen Japan and yet spoke broken English. He knew that he was ashamed of her and he knew that he was thus doubly shamed. He sent a check at the end of every month. The cab screeched into the Airport Departures Terminal. He got out.

He stood at the end of a long line of the Golden-Aged leading to the Air West counter. 'Standby is all we've got,' said the girl. 'You can still have a reserved seat on the ten o'clock flight.' He tried United. They were sold out as well. He put himself on standby with both airlines. He bought himself coffee in a styrofoam cup. It tasted of all the chemistries of modern existence. Two hours later, he was still waiting – squeezed between a fat lady with a transistor radio and a man with bad breath – on the narrow plastic seat provided by the city fathers to speed people on their journey. He called Las Vegas again. It was nearly eight o'clock and Davis was still not there.

Finally, he picked up a No Show on the 9:35 Air West flight and rode with a plane full of red-necked volunteer firemen who wore plastic hats and who cavorted up and down the aisle brandishing fake axes, drinking gallons of cheap, tepid pink champagne, pinching the stewardesses asses, and whooping, 'Put out the fire!'

After what seemed an eternity, the green emerald that was Las Vegas at night swam up under the port wing. They banked, swooped and were down. In the darkness, the hot smell of jet fuel and dry desert air mixed with the swirling gay multitudes swiftly loaded into the hotel buses and borne away to the syndicated gardens of earthly delight.

He paused long enough to call Janet. Her voice was tired, as tired as his. When he told her that he didn't know when he'd be home she said, 'Maybe you shouldn't bother to come home at all.'

'That's a pretty nasty thing to say,' he said.

'It's exactly what I feel at the moment,' she said.

'I love you,' he said.

'Stop reciting it like litany,' she said. 'Eddie — ' She was going to say *I didn't mean that*, but he had hung up.

He got his car out of the airport garage and drove out to the Nevada Operations Office. The guard on the gate looked at his pass and waved him through. Rosen was on the telephone in his office, in his shirtsleeves – which Eddie noticed were very dirty – and he winked. Eddie sat down and listened. Rosen was talking to Hanford and making notes. He was trying to detail the shipping movements as scheduled from their end. He would pause at the end of each note to blow his nose into a Kleenex which he took from a box on his littered desk. Rosen had a cold. It was from working in the air-conditioned smog all day and then spending the night inside his air-conditioned house. Rosen's skin was as pale as a mole's pink face. Eddie wondered how he avoided the sun on weekends. He wondered how a man could live that way.

Rosen finished the call. 'Welcome home,' he said and sneezed. 'That was Hanford. They say that everything was on schedule when the stuff left there. Santa Fe freight car, Number — do you want the number? — Number 3459. Locked, sealed. 6–N containers. Ten of them. Molded pellets. 4.5 kilograms per cask. It was going directly into the fuel rods.'

'Right off the bat,' said Eddie 'Everybody is going to want to know one thing.'

'I know,' said Rosen. 'The consignment was delayed. There was a big stink about it. United Nuclear wanted it right away. Everything else was ready to go and it seems they got on people's backs. Contract crap and all that.'

'So they got it authorized?' said Eddie.

'I guess,' said Rosen. 'No one's about to tell me how?'

'Ten casks in one shipment,' mused Eddie.

' – is a lot of casks,' said Rosen.

'God damn it,' said Eddie.

Rosen looked at Eddie. He rummaged through the drawer of his desk, came up with an open package of Alka Seltzer tablets, took one and chewed it slowly. The clock on the wall said 10:34.

'Could just be that they got stuck somewhere,' said Rosen. 'They had a whopper of a storm up there last night. They're probably just sitting in a siding waiting to get moving again.'

'Somewhere without a telephone,' said Eddie.

'Who knows,' said Rosen. 'It's happened before.' If the remark was intended to ease the tension and give both of them a small sense of security, it failed.

'We both know what has happened before,' said Eddie. 'And that has nothing to do with what is happening now.'

Rosen looked glum. 'Do you want an Alert.'

'Not yet,' said Eddie. 'I think Davis ought to decide that.'

'Well then we just sit,' said Rosen.

'I'm going up to Ogden,' said Eddie. 'I want to find out what the hell is going on.'

'They can be a difficult bunch of people,' said Rosen.

'So can we,' said Eddie. He left the building, stepped into the night and drove back to the airport again. The sky over the strip was green, yellow and red, celebrating the lusts of Man.

He fell asleep on the plane and didn't wake up until it bounced hard coming down.

'Ladies and gentlemen,' said the stewardess. 'Thank you for being with us. Please remain seated until the aircraft reaches the arrivals terminal. Welcome to Salt Lake City. Passengers for Ogden will have twenty-five minutes before re-boarding.' she had a wholesome-sounding voice, the kind that was never tired, angry or anxious.

Eddie got off, found a phone and called the Railroad. He told them that he was coming. He ran out of quarters waiting for the man at the other end to connect him to whoever it was who was in charge. Then it was time to get back on the plane and thirty-five minutes later he was in Ogden. WELCOME TO PIONEER DAYS said a sign hanging from the ceiling inside the terminal. He rented a car and asked directions to the Railroad Yard. He remembered Janet. It was too late to call. The streets of Ogden were deserted. It was two o'clock in the morning. He crossed railroad tracks, saw buildings, floodlights, wire fence, stopped at a gate-house where a guard put a flashlight in his face and asked him what the hell he wanted?

'Pull over there and wait,' he said.

'Look — ' said Eddie.

'Now, you just do as you're told, Mister, or you can turn right around and drive the hell out of here,' said the guard.

'All right,' said Eddie coolly. 'Tell your Yard Superintendent that the man from Las Vegas is here to see him.' He slammed the car into the space and sat in the darkness. There was nothing he could do but that. Sit in the darkness feeling the surges of anger.

The guard sauntered over – flashlight shining in his eyes again. 'Well, it looks like you're OK,' he said. 'Go on in there and park in the visitors' space. That building over there is where you're going. What's your name?'

'Shigata,' said Eddie.

'How do you spell that?'

He spelled it.

'First — '

'Edward.'

'Edward Shigata,' said the guard, writing it in his log. 'Nationality?'

'Japanese-American.'

'Yup,' said the guard. 'Citizen of what country?'

'I was born in the United States,' said Eddie.

'Well — ' said the guard.

'Well, what?' said Eddie.

'Are you a citizen, or ain't you?'

'That's correct,' said Eddie.

'OK,' you can park it,' said the guard. He strolled away.

The Yard Superintendent's Office was on the fourth floor. There were men moving back and forth in the halls. They paused long enough to glance at him, then moved on. 'M. B. Dietrich' said the gold letters painted on the frosted glass. The door to the inner office was open and through it Eddie saw a large, overweight red-faced man wearing a red-striped shirt with big blue suspenders. His coat hung on a pair of deer antlers, his sleeves were rolled up and he was smoking a cigar and sitting in a swivel chair with his feet up on the window ledge behind a huge and ornate oak desk looking down at a line of box cars moving slowly away. He glanced at Eddie and blew smoke at the ceiling. 'What can I do for you?' he said. 'I'm a pretty busy man.'

Eddie nodded. A captain's chair stood under a large photograph of two steam locomotives nose-to-nose surrounded by a crowd of moustachioed men. The silver plaque on the frame said PROMONTORY POINT, 1869. Eddie took the chair and put it next to the desk. He sat down. 'The fact is,' he said. 'I'm a very busy man, myself.'

The feet came down off the window sill. The chair swung around and the small, mean eyes fastened on Eddie. 'Go ahead and say your piece before I have you tossed out of here,' said Dietrich.

'Fine,' said Eddie. 'If that's the way you want it, that's the way it's going to be.' He had had enough. More than enough. 'When I walk out of here, you'll have about an hour to sit there before the Federal Bureau of Investigation moves in. You'll have about two or three more hours to sit there before the owners of this Railroad are informed that they have lost a shipment of strategic nuclear materials for which they are legally responsible. The civil penalties could run into millions of dollars. The criminal penalties — ' Eddie stopped. He stood up and kicked the chair out of the way. 'Or maybe you've heard enough,' he said. 'Maybe you wouldn't like to know what else is going to happen, you son of a bitch!'

'Take it easy,' said Dietrich.

'Where's a goddamned phone,' said Eddie.

'Just take it easy,' said Dietrich. 'You don't want to make any phone calls until you calm down.'

Eddie took a deep, deep breath. The man was right. Whatever else he was, he was right and now he was saying all of the wrong things. Because they had to be said at some point in his life to all of the people who held flashlights in his eyes, and asked him what he was doing inside of his funny, yellow skin.

'That's better,' said Dietrich. 'We're all in this together, now aren't we? I was a little rough on you. It's a habit of mine. Doesn't mean anything personal, I can vouch for that. This is a tough business. Been at it for thirty-six years. Nothing easy about it. Sitting up here I get it from both ends. Sometimes, I wonder why I'm still doing it. I could retire. Let a younger man take over. But the truth is, I love the Railroad. Always have, always will. It gets in your blood. I started out on a survey gang. I spent more of my life in a tent than a house. Canada, Texas, Montana. You name it. There were times when I wished I'd chose some other kind of life, but I didn't.' Dietrich paused. His hand came up with a bottle and two glasses. 'Now what do you say we start all over again? Forgive and forget. That chair – sit down, sit down. Should have offered it to you in the first place – that chair came all the way around Cape Horn during the gold rush and ended up in Cripple Creek, Colorado. Belonged to my grandfather. This is rye whiskey. It's all I drink.' He poured and looked at Eddie.

Eddie reached over and took it.

'If you want water, I can get you some,' said Dietrich.

'No, it's fine,' said Eddie.

'You know, the reason I was so quick on the trigger is because we're about to turn this Railroad upside down looking for that boxcar,' said Dietrich. 'If you know much about railroading, you'd know what I mean.' Dietrich's eyes blinked in the pale, green light of the old cut-glass Pullman lamps hanging over his desk. He looked like a man who worried too much. 'The fellow who should be here to explain it in detail won't be back until tomorrow morning. He's down the line checking things out personally. His name is Mulloy. Chief of Yard Security. If there's anything going on, he'll know about it – or find out.'

The phone rang and Dietrich answered. He handed it to Eddie. It was Chet Davis. He had just returned from Washington. Without preamble he said, 'Any news?'

'I'm afraid not,' said Eddie.

'Then you know what I have to do,' said Davis.

'Maybe wait until tomorrow morning?' said Eddie.

'I'm afraid not,' said Davis. 'They think we've waited too long already.'

'OK, then that's it,' said Eddie.

'You handle things from up there,' said Davis.

'Right,' said Eddie.

'Offer maximum co-operation. They'll need a lot of technical advice. I suppose the Railroad has someone available in a similar capacity?'

'They will,' said Eddie.

'I'm sorry,' said Davis. 'I'll let you know what to do as soon as we get organized.' They both knew what he meant.

Eddie gave the phone back to Dietrich who hung it up.

'Now, as I was saying — ' said Dietrich, swirling the whiskey around in his glass.

'That was my boss,' said Eddie. 'He's ordered an Alert.'

'Now wait a minute. I thought we had agreed to hold off on that,' said Dietrich.

'I'm sorry,' said Eddie. 'The decision wasn't mine to make.'

'Well, then, who the hell's decision was it to make? Your boss? What does he know about what's going on up here? What we're doing?'

'Mister Dietrich, it was the President's National Security Advisor who made the decision,' said Eddie.

'Well, somebody better have some good reasons,' said Dietrich. 'Some damned good reasons.'

'You'll be briefed,' said Eddie.

'By who and for what purpose?'

'By the FBI. The investigation is in their hands now.'

'It's lost,' said Dietrich. 'Just lost.'

'Let's hope so,' said Eddie. 'Let's hope so.'

Somewhere in the darkness a freight train whistled mournfully. Somewhere out there a Santa Fe boxcar was moving.

Chapter Five

The Chief was telling one of his crazy stories about what it was like before the white man came. 'The Utes, the Piutes and the Commanche and the Blackfoot, and it was along about the time of Washakie. And they wanted all of that land up there running between Wind River and Owl Creek and they wanted the gold, too. Lots of gold up there. Indian don't need it. Needs nothing. So they came on in and there must have been a hundred of them. Soldiers with rifles and all of them come from out of the war they just fought against their own brother. So they started killing off the Indian but the Indian don't take it and all them tribes band together and Washakie said, 'We got the same skin, don't we and we got the same reason to fight don't we?' and then off he went and told the white man and they signed a treaty and later on the white man broke it and they went to war. And they killed all the Indians and drove the rest of them so far away they ain't never come back,' said the Chief. Tears rolled down his cheeks. He took a swig out of the bottle and handed it to Arkansas Slim, looked at him out of his sunken eyes and smiled a toothless smile.

'That's what killed you,' said Slim pushing the bottle away. He wasn't in the mood to listen to the Chief. He was too concerned with being watchful and too scared to pay attention to nonsense. From time to time his body twitched involuntarily and that made it even worse. All he needed was to drink some of the Chief's cheap whiskey and listen to some more of the Chief's crazy talk and he would be sitting duck for the ones who were out to get him. And they were no figments of a drunken imagination. They were the two men who had opened up the boxcar where Slim was asleep, letting in the light and the chill of early morning and the silence.

Crazy Talk let out a whoop and a holler.

'You keep still,' hissed Slim. 'Or I'll take away your fire-water and then where will you be?'

'I be better,' said the Chief. 'But worse, too.' The Chief was lying on what was left of the bottom bunk of a Pullman car bed and Slim was next to him peering through the broken window trying to see beyond a dining car that had rolled over on its side. The sun was almost down and the shadows cast by the twisted remnants of all the old passenger equipment that the Railroad had dumped here assumed a kind of grotesque significance. It was a graveyard full of old bones and memory. It was on a siding forty miles south of Jehovah's Junction. It was where Slim had jumped off the freight that had come along just in time to save his skin. Just in time to keep the big one from tackling him in his pell-mell dash for the empty hopper car that would carry him away from that terrible place. His foot still ached where he had kicked him along the side of the head when he made the grab for Slim's leg. It hurt inside the tennis shoes that he had bought at a surplus store to start the summer.

When the door of the boxcar was pulled back he had been as quiet as a rabbit under his blanket in the dark corner. And the man who had opened it had gone off somewhere long enough for Slim to calculate that he was nowhere near Grand Junction, Colorado, which was where he should have been after the long bone-rattling, lurching night aboard the freight that had taken him out of Ogden. And a quick peek around the side of the open door showed him that this was the case. Somehow and for reasons unknown he had ended up at the junction on Massacre Creek which was way out in the middle of the Utah badlands on a stretch of track that went for another hundred miles to nowhere. Three boxcars standing in the early morning sunlight – he could just catch them by sticking out his head. Two Santa Fes and a D&R/

GW. The sound of voices made him pop his head back inside quick and flatten up against the cool steel wall.

At first he couldn't make out what they were saying. Then he could hear but it still didn't make much sense, the words they used and how they spoke. That sort of talk had never made much sense to Slim. A waste of time and intelligence.

The talk went on. Then there was a sharp screech of metal on metal. He knew what that was. They were using a big crowbar on the door of one of the other boxcars. The sound went on until they had snapped off the locks. Then the door was pulled back and they climbed on up inside.

He should have made his break then. But there was nowhere to run except out into the desert. And he knew better than that. There was nothing at all but desert. So he waited for what seemed like an hour with them in that other boxcar making a lot of noise and straining mightily at whatever it was they wanted and indeed they wanted something – Slim knew that – because it wasn't unusual for such things to happen, not on the railroads, which were subject to the same misadventures of mankind as any other system of transportation involved in the movement of valuable goods. Whatever it was they were stealing was none of his business. All he wanted was for them to get it and go. Put in their pick-up truck or whatever they had driven into Jehovah's Junction and depart.

Finally, the noise stopped. He heard them climbing down, the sound in their hard breathing, the astringent smell of human sweat. And from far away, the high note of a train whistle attenuated by the clear air and the distance, but coming closer. It spoke to him, telling him this was his chance.

When it came, he didn't bother with anything. Forty yards separated him from the main line and when he hit the ground he was running. His old legs still had enough in them to make it across that space in high gear and just enough left for him to leap for steel rungs of the ladder on the hopper car. And when the hand had closed around his ankle he had let loose his best kick and connected with it. He hung there on the ladder catching his breath and took a look back.

There were the two of them standing in the dust looking at him as he moved away and there was just one as the train bent around a long curve, moving north toward Grand Junction. The other one had boarded the train. When his strength came back he climbed inside the open car and sat on the shady side. It wasn't all over and done with, yet. That was what he had hoped. One of them was back there at the siding and one of them was following him. Slim had no doubt in his mind at all about what would happen if he should be fool enough to get caught. Whatever it was they were up to, they didn't want people to know. And there was nothing he could tell them to change their minds about his knowing, he could see that from the kind of men they were: one older one and one brawny, wild one and both of them with that look in their eyes that Slim had seen before from time to time in the eyes of other men. Cold-blooded and crazy was what it was.

Then another thought came to him. Charley Greaves. What had happened to old Charley Greaves, the man who threw the switches and sat up in the ancient tower all day long looking at nothing? Maybe old Charley wasn't around anymore. Maybe they had put in automatic switches. But they hadn't. The Junction was the same as always: the switching tower and the shack where Charley lived and the siding with the old loading platforms on one side and the main line on the other. And the old wagon trail that wound around the hill in back and ended where they had buried them – the ones that were massacred a hundred years ago.

By the time he had finished thinking it over Slim was spooked up again. He stuck his head out and took a look. All he saw was boxcars stretched out and moving through the wasteland. He sat until the sun was burning through the top of his head and making the steel too hot to touch. He stood up then and let the wind blow against his face. It helped some but not as much as the hat he usually wore. That was in the pack. And his pack was back there at the

Junction. With the notebooks and his blanket and his rain-
coat and his sweater and a couple of cans of beans – Camp-
bell's Pork and Beans, one of the few things that hadn't
changed in the last sixty-five years. His wallet was where it
always was; strapped to his thigh with thick rubber-bands.
They wouldn't get that. They could read the notebooks all
they wanted but they wouldn't figure them out. There was
no one in the world but himself who could read the pictures.
As soon as he got home to Arizona he would rewrite them
from scratch. Nothing was lost. All he had to do was get to
where he was going. They would never find him there. Even
if they were looking.

Still, when the time came to drop off the freight at the
graveyard, Slim was careful to do it on the blind side of a
curve just outside of the old sidings. He rolled under a big
tumbleweed and lay there until the train was out of sight.

And he had limped into the jumble of old Pullmans,
coaches, dining cars, club cars and other wreckage and
climbed aboard the Pride of St Louis, where he always stayed
when he was in this vicinity. And he had found the Chief –
smelled him, first – bunked down and on one of his thirty-
day drunks – on the warpath, as it were.

Now it was about seven o'clock but he wanted to make
sure. The Chief had an old pocket watch he always carried
so he asked him. The Chief was lying on his back snoring
and when Slim gave him a shake he opened one eye and said:
'Go with you.'

'No, you're not,' said Slim. 'You're staying right here.
Just tell me what time it is and go back to sleep.'

After much hauling and tugging the Chief got out the
watch and after a long consideration of the possibilities, he
announced that it was eleven o'clock in the morning. Slim
grabbed it and turned it right-side-up. It was nearly 7:30.
Time to be moving.

'Now don't you say anything about me being here,' he
told Crazy Talk. 'You do and they'll get you. Understand?'

The Chief's head bobbed up and down. He reached for
his bottle. The last Slim saw of him he had it tilted up and

back like the statue of a thirsty god he had once seen inside
the Metropolitan Museum in New York. Just before they
came and tossed him out for loitering too close to the well-
dressed and well-heeled.

Boarding a freight at night was something Slim didn't
like doing. If you missed, it was easy to roll under the
wheels. He knew quite a few who had done just that. Every
now and then the Railroads would send along a clean-up
crew and sometimes they would find what was left. Usually
it was just bones. The dogs and the coyotes would almost
always get there first.

When the freight came through, he was ready. He spotted
the car he wanted in the moonlight. An empty ore carrier,
the easiest kind to grab for. He ran along with it, reached
up, found the rung of the ladder and swung himself up. In
another half-minute he was sitting inside and looking up at
the stars and all the galaxies of outer space. He was hungry
and tired and cold. But the sight of all that put his visceral
miseries in proper perspective. Whatever is out there couldn't
be any worse than what's down here, he thought. He closed
his eyes and let the cradle of steel rock him to sleep.

Chapter Six

The hamburgers came by catering wagon. They were carried through the parking lot, now full of unmarked government cars, and into the big building that faced the Railroad Yard, leaving the smell of grease and onions in the night air. The men in the nondescript but well-tailored suits stood on the asphalt along with a crowd of Yard workers who ignored them. Whatever it was they were here for, these youngish and belly-heavy strangers with short-clipped hair and the mannerisms of big city places, the Railroad sensed an intrusion, a certain violation of territorial rights, but one which for the moment remained in the abstract.

Inside the building the invaders had taken over the top floor – the entire executive wing – from which they moved back and forth in little sorties aimed at different offices and different people. Occasionally, a group of agents would leave, only to be replaced by another contingent. At other times, a nervous Yard employee would appear, to be ushered through the leather covered double doors into the sacred precincts of the company by thin-lipped, nervous men with expressionless eyes. Inside the building, tension had thrown an iron band around everyone and everything.

Upstairs the agents knew their job: it was to take charge as quickly and efficiently as possible while maintaining the most stringent control over the release of any information that might explain their presence or compromise the investigation.

Therefore, the scenario: It was one of several . . . written in advance, and like all such materials of the imagination,

subject to the talent, intelligence and stage-craft of the per-
formers. Since most of them had not seen the script before
their arrival, a fair amount of confusion was in order. The
only trouble with this was that the curtain was already up, the
footlights of history shining into cigarette smoke-filled rooms
with an audience that could prove to be troublesome if it
discovered that the plot was all illusion, the dialogue a con-
coction, the characters absurd. The opening lines stated that
a shipment of pharmaceutical supplies headed for the Third
World had been lost in transit from Chicago to San Diego.
Not only were the supplies valuable but they contained
dangerous substances including large amounts of narcotic
drugs to be used in clinical applications. The FBI had been
invited to join the search by the Federal Food and Drug
Administration. In such investigations it was common practice to seek the resources, talent and manpower of the
Bureau. It was also common practice to conduct searches
of this nature without informing the public, a policy designed
to prevent irresponsible distortions of facts and events by
the news media. An announcement, if any, of the recovery
could be made at a convenient later date.

Joe Morse hoped the situation might be resolved too
swiftly for any of the dogs to catch the scent. He was the
Agent In Charge – at least for the moment. Knowing the
Bureau as well as he did, he had no doubt that his tenure
would be of brief duration. No one from a Field Office in
Salt Lake City was going to overrule the hierarchy that was
on its way from Washington, DC. And certainly not Joe
Morse whose career assignment was the bush leagues, whose
retirement was only six months away.

For the past thirteen hours he had been the helmsman of a
somewhat rudderless ship adrift on a sea of speculation and
uncertainty. *With full authority to conduct an investigation
into the probable causes of the disappearance of . . .* the voice
on the telephone had said at 4:30 in the morning. And then
the rolling out of bed and the stumbling for the cup of coffee
and the quiet words to his wife, and the long drive up the
highway in the first light of dawn, the truckers pulling off at

cafés where the neon was hard on the edges of the morning and people sat behind the plate glass frozen in a kind of immutable stillness. And then the outskirts of Ogden, mobile homes and trailer parks with washing on the lines, Levis and tee-shirts hanging limp in the still air, and some Gospel preacher on the radio telling the world that Jesus was out there and that He cared. And finally, the Railroad Yard and bleary-eyed men ushering him upstairs where a tired looking Japanese in a rumpled suit told him what had happened, which was pretty simple to understand although not so simple when the Jap launched into the technicalities and even less simple when the guy who ran the Yard tried to explain his side of things. By the time they were through, it was 8:30am and the phone calls had started. Agents from Las Vegas, San Francisco, Los Angeles wanted to know the quickest way into Ogden, wanting to know what it was all about, wanting to know what they should wear – how long it would take.

For the last thirteen hours Joe Morse had spent most of his time dealing with the logistics of his own organization. It was a thankless task and he had had plenty of them since the day of his departure from Washington DC more than twenty years ago . . . the day following his formal rebuke by the Assistant Director of the Bureau who had held the memo that Joe had written in a trembling hand and warned him that opinions such as his on the legalities of Bureau activities were both undesirable and disloyal to the Director, himself. That, perhaps, he should seriously consider a career in some other aspect of law enforcement. The memo had been shredded and Joe had been reassigned to Minnesota. He had become a member of the remittance gang . . . as the men of the far-flung outposts of the Empire called themselves. Since coming to Utah nine years ago, his biggest case had been the arrest of a ring of cattle rustlers who used a van to truck the cows to a slaughterhouse in Nevada where they were converted to hamburger for a second-rate chain of fast-food restaurants, long since gone out of business. He wondered, though, if maybe they hadn't made a comeback as he chewed on what one of the boys from LA put in front of him and washed it down with what passed for coffee.

The phone rang again. It was from the agent assigned to find motel space for at least fifty people. He wanted to know if $14 a day was a fair price? Joe told him that it was and reminded him that he had another chore – to rent as many cars as he could find so that the arriving forces would be able to move at will on their appointed rounds. The agent wanted to know if someone else could do that? Joe told him that he would see what he could do, but to go ahead.

The door to the big office that he was using swung open and the Yard Superintendent Dietrich was ushered in. He sank down into the proffered chair.

'I think we're on to how it happened,' he said.

'How — ?' said Morse.

'Routing indicator foul up,' said Dietrich.

'What is a routing indicator?' said Morse.

'It codes the car through the automated switching grid which is controlled by the computer. What that means is that when the car goes over the hump it's sequenced according to what is on the tape,' said Dietrich.

'So, what happened?' asked Morse.

'The car didn't go through right,' said Dietrich.

'I would have assumed you knew that already,' said Morse.

'Railroading is a complex business, Mister Morse. You don't assume anything until you've proved it.'

'That's our policy, too,' said Morse. 'Just where in your opinion would a boxcar go if an event occurred such as the one you just described?'

'Every yard, depot and siding in this division is being checked,' said Dietrich. 'If it's out there, we'll find it.'

'Maybe you could use some help from us,' said Morse.

'I think we're handling it pretty well,' said Dietrich.

'You mind me asking how many men that involves?'

'Hard to say. Two, maybe three hundred. If it's there we'll find it.'

'And if you don't?' Morse said.

'Then it's gone on to some other right of way,' said Dietrich.

Morse had the suspicion that the Yard Superintendent fervently hoped that this was the case.

'It could have gone to Grand Junction. Or the other way, into Nevada. Might even have gone North again,' said Dietrich. There's a lot of truck out there. A lot of boxcars, too.'

'How many boxcars?' said Morse.

'No way of knowing for sure. Maybe twenty, thirty thousand,' said Dietrich. 'That's out of about a million total.'

'You're telling me that there are a million boxcars out there?'

'I'm not telling you. That's how many there are.' said Dietrich. 'Sure, some of them get lost. And some of them get sent the wrong direction. So does everything else in this world. All I can tell you is that we're doing our best and I told you that this morning. I'm going back to my office now. You want me that's where I'll be.'

Morse said nothing. He watched him go. A man who had been up all night was no one to start arguing with. He knew that.

The telephone rang again. He answered.

'This is Matthiessen,' said a brisk voice. 'We've just landed at Hill Air Force Base. We'll be right in. Anything to report?'

'Nothing that can't wait until you're here,' said Morse.

'I see. I thought perhaps you might have done a little better than that,' said Matthiessen. He hung up.

By the time they arrived, the twenty-five of them in their expensive suits and beefy faces, Morse had cleared off the desk. He wanted the transition to be smooth. He realized without shame that he wanted the men from Washington, DC to take over, to run the show. He was too old to pretend, anymore, that he cared very much one way or another about the things that were supposed to matter.

While he was waiting, the phone rang again. It was Dietrich. 'Found a man of ours dead down in Massacre Creek,' he said. 'My Security Chief, he found him. Got the

Sheriff down there looking into it. Thought you might want to know.'

'I'd like to talk to your security man,' said Morse.

'So would I,' said Dietrich. 'I told him to get back here fast, the son of a bitch. He had no orders to go down there in the first place.

Chapter Seven

The boxcar stood next to the open maw of the scrap smelter. The rusted rails died there. It was the end of the track that led up from the Lodestone siding and across the wasted buttocks of the Salmon Valley, a barren land of slag heaps, treeless ridges and abandoned mine workings. The silver was gone. The mines had closed. The valley remained. Not even the Ute Indians wanted it back.

The smelter had a government contract. It melted scrap for the Bureau of Reclamation. The Bureau of Reclamation picked up the scrap from government-owned lands where it had been dumped and abandoned by a vast assortment of Americans, living and dead. The scrap came in on flatcars, boxcars and any other railroad cars deemed fit for such assignments. It came in all shapes and sizes. When melted, it was formed into crude ingots and loaded into ore carriers and sent to Boise. What happened to it after that, nobody at the A and B Industries Smelter knew or cared. The contract made them a living; it was a tiny piece of pork out of the Congressional barrel, more gristle than meat.

'That's what I'm telling you!' the foreman shouted over the rush and whine of helicoptered air. His face was sun-reddened and hostile. In front of him stood a man in a business suit, his jacket flapping wildly. The man nodded, turned, ran back to the aircraft. There was a hurried radio consultation between the men inside and the men in the second helicopter which had appeared and was flying rapidly up the valley. The foreman stood and watched all of this with amazement. The two other men who worked at the smelter came out from the big corrugated iron shed that housed the furnace and stood beside him.

'What's going on?' asked one of them.

'Something about the stuff out of that boxcar,' said the foreman. 'I told them it's already being melted down.'

The man that he had told came running toward them. 'Come on,' he said.

'Come on where?' said the foreman, edging back.

'We've got to get you out of here,' said the man.

The three smelter employees looked at each other.

'Look,' said the man. 'You want to die? Then just stay right there.'

'What the hell is going on?' said the foreman.

'We'll tell you when you get aboard. Come on,' said the man.

Reluctantly, they followed him, ran under the rotors in a crouch and climbed through the door. The helicopter took off. It rose high and circled toward the far side of the valley. The second helicopter came down in the same spot. Three men carrying black cases with metal handles jumped out and ran toward the smelter. The one in front was Eddie Shigata. The other two were from the Nevada Operations Office. They were part of the Nuclear Emergency Search and Recovery Team. As they ran toward the smelter shed the helicopter fled to the safety of the skies.

The big bay doors were open. Eddie ran through, from the bright daylight into the darkness and the heat, the smell of molten metal, the steady roar of the blast furnace. It was at the far end, glowing white hot through the open fire doors. A much closer approach would be necessary, he knew that.

The other two had caught up. 'If it's in there you know where it will be, right smack at the bottom,' said the one with the glasses.

'What if it hasn't been in there long enough,' said the other one. 'It could still be up on top.'

'Let's go,' said Eddie. He flipped open his case, plugged the photomultiplier into the scintillation counter and turned it on. The others did the same. They moved across the concrete floor picking their way through a rusty jungle of scrap waiting for its Armageddon. There was no time for thought. The little needles occupied his attention. They danced and jittered on the scale, as indecisive as butterflies, showing nothing but background count. When they were half-way there Eddie stopped.

'It could be damped off,' he said. He was thinking of the tons of metal inside the furnace. Iron, steel and God knew what, a sluggish, molten mass, absorbing any neutrons, shielding the plutonium – melted gobbets sinking slowly through the incandescent soup to come together at the bottom under incredible extremes of temperature and pressure.

'Well, if it is, there's nothing we can do about it,' said the man with the glasses. What he meant was that they would never know. He walked toward the blast furnace, holding the detector at arms length. Eddie and the other one followed until all of them were stopped by a wall of heat twenty feet from the open doors.

'Around the side!' shouted Eddie. They moved at right angles until they were clear of the doors. They started forward and got ten feet closer. That was the end of the line. It was close enough. The meters trembled. They were holding on background levels. There was nothing more they could do. If it was there, no one could do anything about it.

'Let's get out of here,' said Eddie. They ran. Back to the light, the cool air, the desolation. It was kind of funny, thought Eddie. But if you had to pick a place for something like this to happen, this would be it. If there was plutonium in the furnace and there was enough, when it melted to the bottom it would go critical. Next to a weapon, the furnace was a crude way of igniting an atomic explosion. He wondered what the yield might be? It was interesting to think about that, standing there. Should one run? Should one shout? He would have to take that up with the boys at Livermore. The weapons freaks. *Suppose this. Given ninety pounds of plutonium at the bottom of a blast furnace* . . .

Both helicopters landed, their jet engines winding down into a silence accented by distant echoes that sounded like secret and absurd laughter. In seconds men were all over the place and the foreman was standing in front of Eddie saying, 'I don't know what this is all about but them barrels was empty.'

'How do you know that?'

'Because the tops were broken off. Funny looking on that inside. Rigged up to carry something. Germs, maybe. That what it was?' said the foreman.

'I suppose so,' said Eddie. The reaction was setting in, now. He felt shaky and drained-out.

'Well, whatever it was, one thing's for sure.'

'What's that?'

'It won't be live now. Not in there,' said the foreman. 'Hot enough to melt down anything.'

An agent came trotting over. 'The boss would like to have you report to him personally,' he told Eddie.

Howard Matthiessen stood with his arms folded on the empty flatcar that faced the chimney stack of the blast furnace. He was tall, with silver hair and could have been someone's golf partner at any exclusive club where men of a similar type would gather. He wore a gabardine suit and sunglasses. His stomach was still a little queasy from the two hours of ridge-hopping up to this godforsaken place but his mind was calm. To be on hand – in the thick of it – that was something for the Bureau to know. That Howard Matthiessen was totally in charge.

When the Japanese fellow approached he started to climb up on the flatcar. Matthiessen waved him back down. 'Just the report,' he said. 'No chit chat.'

'We were lucky,' said the Japanese.

'I'm not interested in your opinions,' said Matthiessen. 'What happened?'

The Japanese looked up at him. 'Nothing. The stuff wasn't

in there. If it had been, there would have been a meltdown, an explosion or both.'

'Thank you. That's all,' said Matthiessen. He turned away, ending the interview. But there was one more thing to say. 'Excellent work, Shigata, is it? We in the Bureau appreciate that.'

The Japanese nodded. He moved away. There was going to be trouble with him, Matthiessen could sense it. He had a keen sense of smell for the problematical types. It was better to know them in advance. There were plenty of them in Washington. The non-team players. The ones that undermined investigations and caused trouble.

During the next hour he watched his men swarm over the boxcar dusting for fingerprints. There were thirty-two identifiable sets and more being lifted when Matthiessen reached a decision. He beckoned. An agent came on the double.

'I'll be returning to headquarters. Keep me informed,' he said.

'Yes, sir,' said his man.

'And make sure those nuclear people keep out of your way,' he added.

The flight back to Ogden was uneventful. By the time they landed at the Air Force base, Matthiessen had radioed his instructions. He was driven in a government car to the Railroad Yard. He was escorted upstairs and into one of the conference rooms. There were several men waiting. They were all vice-presidents of the Railroad. They all stood when he entered.

'Now, gentlemen, what we have to determine is, the responsibility for what has happened,' said Matthiessen.

The antique stationmaster's clock clicked softly in the silence. The time was 11:32am.

In San Diego it was one hour earlier. When the doorbell

rang, Margie Acosta was sitting on the small patio behind the tract-built house. Getting up, she spilled the bourbon she had been drinking. There were two men outside. She eyed them from behind the screen door.

'We're looking for a Mrs Acosta,' said the one on the left. 'My name is Burke and this is Mr Childress.'

'What do you want?'

'Just to ask you a few questions. It's about your father, George Sims.'

'We had that already. When he went to work as a security guard. Is that what it's about?'

'Well, not exactly. You see, we're from the Department of Health, Education and Welfare,' said the one on the right.

'You wouldn't have any proof of that?'

'Of course,' said the one on the left. Both men held up their wallets and flipped them open. 'We'd like to come in,' he said.

'I'm a little busy at the moment.'

'We're really very sorry to intrude but the matter is rather urgent.'

'That's what they all say,' said Margie. She unlatched the screen door and told them, 'Out there.' She led them to the patio. They all sat down.

'I've always loved patios,' she said. 'Even postage stamp ones.'

'Could I ask you where your husband is?'

'Where the hell do you think he is? He's at work.'

'At the bakery?'

'Yes, at the lousy bakery. How did you know that?'

'It was in your father's file. His medical records.'

'Something the matter with him? Is that why you're here?'

'Not that we know of. It's just that from time to time in his work he might come into contact with contagious materials.'

'Some job,' she said. 'At least it keeps him out of the house.'

'How long has he lived with you?'

'Since he came out from Florida. That was a laugh. Said

he wanted to see his grandchild before he died. Said he was coming for a week. That was eight years ago. You know what he does? All he does when he's home is sit around telling you how good Florida was and how sorry he is he ever decided to move out here. And then he starts on the Communists, the Jews and Niggers. Well, my husband he comes from a Cuban background so you can imagine what that's like for him. If it wasn't for the fact that my sister wouldn't put up with him, he wouldn't be here. She's the one with the money. She married this tax lawyer for a big corporation. They won't have anything to do with him at all. And I'll tell you why,' said Margie, pouring herself another drink.

'What we would like to know — ' said the man named Childress.

' — is why the hell we put up with it?' said Margie. 'That's a good question. Another thing he does is, he brings home his friends from the American Legion. They sit around here drinking beer and watching wrestling matches. You should hear them. According to them, half the damned country ought to be given back to the Indians. Not that they like the Indians. Their big hero is J. Edgar Hoover.'

'Maybe you could tell us if your father has any other friends?' said Childress. 'People from Florida.'

'Who knows and who cares.'

'Maybe someone in the Cuban community?'

'Well I wouldn't know about that. What's it got to do with his medical records?'

'Just background,' said Childress.

'All of his people came from Pennsylvania. For what they were worth. I grew up there. The only thing we ever did was go to Atlantic City on the Fourth of July. My mother was afraid of her own shadow. The doctors said it was something wrong with her thyroid glands. She wouldn't leave the house. You can imagine what that was like. I'm going to tell you what it was like,' said Margie. 'I didn't feel like talking to anybody, today, but now that you're here, I'm glad you stopped by.'

'Maybe we could — ' said Childress.

'Don't interrupt me. You'll get your chance,' said Margie. She started to pull out her hair curlers.

The Garvey Hotel was downtown, under the landing pattern to the San Diego Municipal Airport. Every time a jet landed, the building shook and the noise drowned out the television set in the corner of the small lobby. None of the men sitting on the vinyl-covered couches watching the daytime soap operas paid any attention. 'Oh, sure,' the clerk was saying. The rest of it was lost in the thunder of an arriving plane. When the noise had passed he went on, 'One of the nice ones. He's lived here for maybe three years. Spends his time at the museums a lot. Watches birds, too, I think.' He came around from in back of the desk and led the two men over to the small elevator. On the way up he said: 'Never said anything about having to guard anything that could have hurt him.' They got off on the fifth floor. 'This is it. His room. Marcus Whittaker,' said the clerk, unlocking the door. 'Hear those bells? It's the Mission. Ring them a lot. But you can't usually hear them,' he said.

Chapter Eight

Mulloy found him about three o'clock in the afternoon. He had gone up there expecting to find him but it took him a little time to face up to the idea. The cicadas were singing. It was a dirge for Charley Greaves. He was lying face-down covered up with dirt up at the old cemetery where they'd buried the Mormons. He was there stuck right on top of Julia Adams – so said the cross. He was a nice old guy. Never worried about anything. Never would again. The back of his head was all bashed in.

Down at the shack where he had lived there was a calendar with a picture of some south seas island. Charley had marked off the days on it. In the shed out back there was a pick and a shovel. He used them to break up the hard pan every spring for his garden. Someone had used the shovel before the sun had burned the dew off.

The garden was next to the water tower. This year it didn't amount to much. The sun had killed his squash. The Tomatoes looked thirsty so Mulloy turned on his gravity-fed sprinkler and watched the water cascade down over the neat rows and disappear into the thirsty earth. He wanted to stay there, maybe even take off his clothes and stand in the middle of it. He didn't want to go looking for Charley. It was like knowing that you would take a woman to bed and knowing that her arms and legs would encircle you no matter what was said. The anguish was in the knowing. All in the knowing.

So, Mulloy poked around for a long time. He climbed up in the tower and sat in Charley's old horsehair chair looking down at the tracks and out across the desert. There was no wind yet and no sound but the sound of his own breathing. Finally, he got down and headed up the old road taking the shovel. He knew Charley was up there. Where else would you put somebody in a place like this if you took the trouble to put him anyplace at all? That didn't explain how he knew, but it was as good as anything else.

And when Mulloy found him he stood there for a while, a little dizzy, a little tired, wanting the clean sheets that Pearl always had on the big, brass bed. Nothing fancy – just clean, white sheets. And she would be getting up now, he thought. It was her time. The time when all the whores got up. Not that she had to do it. Only when she wanted and who she wanted. Advantages of ownership. Prerogatives of the long, hard life.

Now the wind had come up to blast the tombstones and shake the dead grasses and to rattle at his pantlegs. He got Charley up out of the ground and sat him up. He took off his own coat and slung Charley over his shoulder. It was a good half mile back down and into the teeth of the wind. When Mulloy got Charley home a fine white powder of dust had covered both of them. He put Charley in his bed and sat himself down on the corner of the dirty mattress. They stared at each other and then Charley's alarm clock jangled. It was still set for five in the morning. Charley had never turned it off. Mulloy did.

He left him there and walked up the tracks carrying his valise. There was no one he could call because Charley's telephone was as dead as he was. Someone had cut the line in about five places. He was heading for a pile of railroad ties to sit down and wait for the next freight when he saw the knapsack. It was lying in the dirt and there was nothing inside it but a pair of old wool socks and the notebooks. Mulloy didn't have to open them up because he knew who they belonged to and what they were: old Slim's testaments to his travels. Little pictures of the way things were. Mulloy wondered if he was in there, somewhere? Perhaps he was the stick-figure with the coyote's head . . . or the devilish-looking face that peered through an abstracted boxcar door? He had certainly thrown Slim out of enough of them over the last twenty years. Finally, he had just let him be.

It took about an hour for the train to come through and by that time he was pretty drunk.

Mulloy stood in the middle of the track and waved the locomotive down. The pissed-off engineer yelled, 'What the hell do you think you're doing!'

'Getting on the goddamn train!'

Mulloy showed him his ID. He handed it back down. He was a young one.

'Well fuck your brother,' he said.

'Screw you, too,' Mulloy said, and he trotted for the caboose.

'You could've got yourself killed,' shouted the train driver.

Never mind, never mind what anyone says, including yourself, he thought. It was all a lot of bullshit, anyway, the whole grimy mess of it. He slipped on a tie and fell down. Finally he made it to the end of the freight where the train conductor cast disapproving glances upon him. Mulloy said he was sorry to cause him a delay and the guard asked where Charley was and was there something wrong with him.

'When did you come through here last?' said Mulloy.

The morning, like always. Around 4:30.'

'Drop off or pick up anything?'

'As a matter of fact, two ... three empties.'

'Santa Fe stuff?'

'Yeah, I think a couple of them was.' A ripple of movement passed down the boxcars and then hit them with a savage jerk. 'Yeah, there was a couple of them, all right. Charley would have told you that. You sure he's all right?'

'Well, he's got a headache,' said Mulloy.

'He ought to have some aspirin for that,' said the train conductor. He went inside and Mulloy sat on the platform.

There was one belt left in the bottle and Mulloy took it, watching the Junction disappear. He stood up and threw the bottle at a telegraph pole. It missed. He went inside. The guard was sitting there shuffling through his waybills.

'Wouldn't have any idea where those cars went?' said Mulloy.

'No, by God, I don't,' said the guard.

'You going through the Junkyard?' The guard nodded. 'Then wake me up when you get there,' said Mulloy.

And he did.

Mulloy hit the cinders. On the wrong leg again. They glittered by the moonlight. The freight slithered away until all that was left was a red light occulting into nothing. He went through the hole in the fence and into the bone yard – the memories and the junk. They always made him think of the same thing: Big Ben lifting him up, putting him aboard, saying, 'It's all right, Jacky-boy, I'll see you in a few days.' Chair cars and hotel rooms and towns where the meanness was rooted in every glance, where they beat you up bad the first day of school and you never went back anymore even when Ben told you: 'Do you want to end up like me? Do you want to end up a lousy yardbull or do you want to amount to something?' Ben with his worn out tweed suit, his worn out Irish brogue, and celluloid collars lying in his coffin the day the Railroad buried him with the bullet in his head from his own gun put there by God knows who somewhere between Boise and Pocatello, where they found him dead in the boxcar. Those were rough times, he thought. We all search for our fathers and end up finding only ourselves.

The Indian was lying face-down in a pool of his own blood, vomit and excrement. Someone had done a fancy job of cutting him up. And then, when they were through, graffitied his forehead with the point. SINNER, said the red lines. Mulloy went outside of the Pullman car where he was lying and threw up, too. When that was over he went back in and poked around with his flashlight. There was nothing except the flotsam and jetsam of the years. And the carrion of the moment. 'Sorry, Chief,' he mumbled and left him there and hiked over to the highway stumbling on the hard edges of the shale.

He waved his flashlight at a car. It sped up. So did the next and the next and the next. Finally, a Hell's Angel type came along and skidded his motorcycle to a full stop on the soft shoulder of the road. He sat on his bike and took a good look at Mulloy. He nodded and Mulloy climbed up behind him. Without a word they took off. The night rushed by and they came to the town of Terminus. There was an all-night diner at the far end of the only paved street and the motorcycle stopped there. Mulloy got off and his friend roared away. He went inside, had a cup of coffee, and called the local sheriff's office.

He spent what was left of the night in a Maw-and-Paw motel listening to the bugs hit the porch light and waiting sleeplessly for the dawn. He got out of Terminus at 10:30 in the morning on a freight headed for Grand Junction. That was where old Arkansas was headed. It was where they all headed to lay over between trains and it was where the old man had to go if he wanted to catch something heading south, toward the Mexican border. Mulloy's only hope was that he would catch up with him before somebody else did. On such thoughts he dwelled as the freight train passed through the desert under the bright blue mirror of the sky. It was easier to think about that than about what Dietrich had said when Mulloy had called him from the Terminus Dispatch Office.

Dietrich had said, 'Get back here now or you can turn in your tin badge with this company.'

Mulloy had answered, 'I'm on to something.'

Dietrich had laughed, 'You're on to nothing. We found the boxcar and it's empty.'

Chapter Nine

Howard Matthiessen stood in front of the portable black-board like the corporate president he might have been. All of the men in the room had scratch pads and pens. Their white shirt-sleeves were rolled up to a point just below their elbows and those who didn't smoke chewed gum and longed for what they had given up. In the days ahead suits would be rumpled, collars stained with nervous sweat, shoes un-polished and tempers would hover on the ragged edge. Exhaustion, tension and frustration would bloom like the algae drifting on the red tides of summer, a creeping toxin that would saturate the tissues of the brain.

'Now, gentlemen,' said Howard Matthiessen, tapping the blackboard with his pointer. 'I think we all understand the methodology that will be implemented in this investigation. You will coordinate your activities with the technical sup-port people if and when necessary. Steer clear of local law enforcement unless otherwise notified. We can't afford to run the risk of inadvertent disclosures, at least not at this point. If you have to deal with them use the dangerous drug cover. Anything you turn up, anything at all, must be reported to the headquarters team immediately. At other times check in when it's possible. You men in the field will be the spearheads of this operation. We're depending on you to provide us with the information that will lead to a successful recovery of the missing material. I need not say that the highest level of performance is expected from each and every one of us, nor add that the issues involved in this situation are potentially embarrassing to a large number of people. So, do your best, men. Thank you.'

They all rose as he left.

Joe Morse stood up with the rest of them. It was a ritual celebrating nothing, the show of unity as mandatory to the Bureau's activities as its outmoded codes of dress and behavior: lip service to the chivalric era of mighty men and mighty deeds, to Tommy guns and John Dillinger. The Boss was still watching. For some of them he wasn't even dead. Or, like the Dali Lama, had been reincarnated in the flesh of the man now leaving the room.

Other men took his place. They gave specific details, assigned specific tasks, answered questions, developed theories. Joe Morse had flown B-25s during the War. It was the same. Except that then, all of them knew that some of them wouldn't be coming back from Hamburg or Dresden or other pinpoints on the map.

'Now, gentlemen, we have a massive amount of territory to cover and a massive amount of data to analyze,' said the last man to hold the pointer. 'We know that a diversion has occurred and we know that there is a high degree of probability that this operation was planned well in advance by persons with radical motives. We don't know what those motives are, at least not at present. We do know that the security arrangements for the shipment were subverted in a manner yet to be determined and we have reason to believe that this involved at least one of the two men aboard that train. Investigations of their background are proceeding parallel to your own. Any more questions?'

Someone asked, 'How dangerous is this stuff?'

'Don't eat it, breathe it or stick it in your underwear,' said the man with the pointer. Everyone laughed. 'Otherwise we've been assured that it represents no significant hazard over a short period of time. There *is* one other thing, gentlemen. Under no circumstances should you attempt to collect the material in any kind of container. This could result in a radiation hazard with possibly serious effects.'

Someone said, 'What about a bomb?'

The man with the stick smiled: 'That, gentlemen, would take months of preparation. And years of training.'

Someone said, 'What would be the motive then?'

'We don't know, gentlemen. Blackmail or profit. Possibly both. Plutonium is worth $18,000 a gram. Selling it wouldn't be hard in certain parts of the world. I think that's the greatest risk,' said the man with the pointer. He was only repeating what he had been told, what the experts said. No questions entered his mind or the minds of the men in front of him.

The meeting broke up. The men automatically crumpled their notes and dumped them in the big canvas mailbag that had been brought from the Operations Center mailroom and which now stood inside the door. The paper shredder that had been requisitioned had not yet arrived.

There were certain other logistical problems. Joe Morse was drafted to help sort them out. He was put in charge of moving the accumulated computer print-outs from the Operations Center upstairs to a conference room where a team of programmers had gathered to sort out the 37,682 separate boxcar movements that had taken place in the Utah, Nevada, Wyoming and Idaho region during the twenty-four hour period during which the Santa Fe boxcar had deviated from its charted course.

Then he was put in charge of moving the accumulated employee records of the railroad from the personnel office downstairs and into two waiting government vans which would take them to Hill Air Force Base from which place they would depart to Washington, DC where routine comparisons would be made with Justice Department records, a euphemism for the National Crime Information Files. If the legality of these proceedings was questionable it was a nicety that no one chose to examine. The Railroad employed twelve thousand people. The names in the files with the attached remarks that were buried in the megaliths of the governing bureaucracy had become the population of another country, a polity of ghosts indexed according to their sins in life waiting for final disposition, whatever that would be. Joe Morse's duty was to ferry this new batch of souls across the parking lot to the trucks. When they were gone he stood and listened to the freight train whistles.

Five minutes later he was assigned to follow up on a peripheral matter – a call from the city desk of the Ogden Standard. The paper wanted to know what all the activity at the Railroad Yard was about, or so said the woman at the reception desk who had been told to refer any such calls to Joe. 'They say they heard there was an accident,' she said. 'Is that what it is? Is that what all these men are doing?'

Joe told her he would take care of it.

'Nobody ever tells me anything,' she said.

He called the newspaper back and talked to the city editor. He knew the local press. It was easy-going, conservative and not much interested in what was happening in the rest of the world. It ran William Buckley and Ronald Reagan on the editorial page and exalted the traditions of the pioneers. The city editor was an oldtimer named Atkins. He had once worked for the *Salt Lake City Tribune*. That was as far as he'd gotten. Maybe he didn't want to go any further. Joe didn't ask what he was doing up here. He told him that they were doing a security survey of Railroad Operations, that it was a purely routine procedure, that nothing else was going on.

'Then I guess it isn't worth sending anybody over,' said Atkins.

'I wouldn't think so,' said Joe Morse.

'Thought maybe it was about that killing down in Massacre Creek.'

'Afraid not. What was that about?' said Joe Morse.

'Fellow got himself killed.'

'That's what you already said.'

'Didn't amount to much. It was just some old guy they kept down there to throw the switches. It's half-way to hell and gone, way out in the middle of nowhere. Anyway, someone gave it to him with the back of a shovel. Got the story from the Sheriff's office down there. Whoever did it would have had to come in on a freight. Or drop out of the sky and climb back up again. The Sheriff was pretty het up about it. Coming in there and killing an old man like that. He's about to start a long-haired-hippie-drug-fiend hunt. Hell's Grannies is about all he'll find in those canyons. They don't have much of that either down there.'

'When did it happen?' asked Joe.

'Night before last,' said Atkins. 'Mulloy found him.'

'He's the security guy who works up here isn't he?'

'When he isn't drinking he's OK,' said Atkins. 'Wonder what the hell he was doing down there? Whenever he gets off he usually goes down to Nevada.'

'And — ?' said Morse.

'And comes back,' said Atkins.

Morse didn't press it. Journalists had their sources to protect. He had his.

'Anyway, the story is in this afternoon's paper,' said Atkins. 'Page two. We don't run stuff like that up front during Pioneer Days. Might scare off the tourist trade. Make them head for Disneyland.'

'You're just a cynic,' said Joe.

'Oh, I don't know. Sometimes I think that what's going on in the world has nothing to do with what's going on inside people's heads.'

'I guess you're right about that,' said Joe.

'Of course I am,' said Atkins.

'Give me a call if you get down to Salt Lake sometimes and I'll buy you a drink,' said Joe.

They both laughed. It was an old joke. There weren't any bars in Salt Lake City. The Mormons took it in teacups if they took it at all.

'Well, as long as you're out there at the Yard you can do me a favor,' said Atkins.

'Sure,' said Joe.

'Tell that fellow in the scheduling office to stop writing those letters. I'm getting tired of reading them,' said Atkins. 'Maybe coming from you it will make him think twice.'

'Sure,' said Joe. 'What is he saying?'

'Practically nothing. Claims the world is coming to an end

sometime this week or the next – don't remember which. Wants us to publish the good news. So that folks will get down on their knees and start praying before it happens. I've been getting a letter a day from him for the last couple of months. You'd think he'd have something better to do than that. Don't want to get him in any trouble. Just a word from the wise if you know what I mean,' said Atkins. 'Name of Jarvis. George Jarvis.'

'Sure. I'll see what I can do,' said Joe.

He drifted through the harrassed legions of his fellow agents downstairs to the personnel office. It was a shambles of emptied file cabinets and upset women. He asked if anyone knew of a George Jarvis? A woman with pink fingernails, orange hair and violet-tinted contact lenses said that there was somebody by that name, she thought, who worked in the freight scheduling office. 'He'd be in the records.' She cast a baleful eye upon him. 'It's going to take us weeks to straighten this out. I hope you appreciate that,' she said. He appreciated it.

Upstairs again, he plunged into the maelstrom of the disrupted operations center, found someone who told him to talk to someone else who pointed toward an office. Inside was a crew-cutted man yelling at the telephone about a shipment of insecticide that somebody in North Dakota was waiting for and a shipment of Cadillacs that a lot of people were waiting for. He hung up and glared at Joe Morse. He said, 'What the hell do you want?'

'Is there a Jarvis working here?'

'No.'

'You know where he works?'

'No. Wait a minute. Try the scheduling office.'

'Where's that?'

'Downstairs. In the basement.'

The basement was full of computers, computer terminals, and computer people. Computer people were as faceless and interchangeable as the machines they worked with: the functions of functions. He was thinking this while the man who knew George Jarvis was saying, 'A week and a half ago. I can't remember the day. Maybe it was Friday.'

'Why did he quit?' said Joe.

'Never said. He never said much about anything, anyway.'

'How long did he work here?'

'Longer than me. He was here when I came. That was two and a half, three years ago.'

'What was his job?'

'Scheduling.'

'What's that involve?'

'Putting numbers into the computers, mostly. Sometimes you write a new program. That usually comes down from Denver. We do it here, too. It all gets sent upstairs to operations. Yeah, old George was a kind of a funny guy.'

'How so?'

'Well, he got religious. Anything he had to say, it was always, the Lord this, the Lord that. I'm not against it, myself, but it didn't have much to do with the job.'

'What church?'

'Wouldn't know.'

'Wouldn't know where he lives?'

'Wouldn't know that either. You'd have to try the personnel office. That's upstairs. Second floor.'

'I know,' said Joe Morse.

'Used to read a lot when he wasn't busy.'

'Anything in particular?'

'The Bible. Book of Revelations. Used to quote it, chapter and verse. Fire and brimstone and all that. You wouldn't believe it, some of that stuff in the Bible. Try them up in Personnel. They ought to know how to get in touch with him.'

He waited for the elevator. It was just something to check out. A possibility, as remote as any other. Something to go on because it was better for him than standing still. He punched the button again, fumbled for a cigarette. But the guy had quit a couple of weeks ago, he thought. That seemed to rule him out completely. The damned elevator was stuck somewhere. He took the fire stairs. Anyway, he would have a word with Matthiessen. If Matthiessen would listen. He reached the first floor and opened the door and the lobby was full of men, full of agents leaving, carrying out armloads of their stuff, a migrating army of them, a plague of button-down-collared locusts eating up the world and spewing it back out.

He chased one out the door and asked him what was going on. The man looked at him like he was an idiot. 'We've broken it,' he said.

'What?' said Joe Morse. 'What do you mean?'

'One of the guards,' said the agent. 'They found one of the guards.'

'So?'

'The other one wasn't with him.'

'What did he say?'

'Nothing. He was dead.'

'Where's the boss?'

'Headed for the airport. We're moving down to Las Vegas.' Joe was about to ask him some more questions when one of Matthiessen's men saw him, came over and said, 'Been looking for you. You've been assigned to wrap things up here. We're moving the investigation down to our own office in Las Vegas. Check in with us if anything important happens. Mostly, I think you'll be soothing ruffled feathers, maintaining liaison – that sort of thing.'

'Sure,' said Joe Morse. 'So it was one of the guards?'

'That's what it looks like. They hire a lot of yoyos. This one was no yoyo.'

'Which one was it?'

'Haven't had a chance to find out, myself. All I knew is they found the other one.'

'Where?'

'Canada,' said Matthiessen's man and he walked away.

Ten minutes later they were all gone. Joe Morse was walking down an empty hallway littered with empty coffee cups and sandwich wrappers. He sat down at the desk in the office where he had started twenty-four hours ago. Years ago the tidal wave of the War had rushed through the islands

of the South Pacific leaving him in its wake to sort the dead
and broken, to tell the natives that no more fire would come
from the sky. It was like that again for Joe Morse. The world
was running out from under him more quickly than he could
guess.

Chapter Ten

The body on the mortuary table lay naked and alone. Consciousness had escaped it leaving the flesh behind in a purgatory of red tape, enough to carpet any stairway to heaven. A corridor beyond the swinging doors led to the Victorian living room. This room served as the chapel for the deceased and departed citizens of Indian Head, Saskatchewan, population: 182. There a mounted policeman, a constable and the senior US Consulate Officer from Winnipeg, Manitoba, stood in front of the bay windows, looking through the lace curtains at the thunderheads which filled the horizon.

'I'm sorry, but the law is the law,' the mounted policeman was saying for the tenth time. 'We cannot turn him over to you until his identity is established and an autopsy is performed to certify cause of death. I wish I could speed things up but I'm hardly in a position to do so, sir.'

'I quite understand,' said the man from the Consulate. 'My instructions are to assist you by offering you the fullest co-operation of our own law enforcement agencies – in a purely advisory capacity, of course.' He yawned unintentionally. It was 96° outside and humid. He had driven the 260 miles from Winnipeg alone to deliver the message. Whatever the hell was going on, he had been told by Washington, was none of his business. How they had found out about the dead man in Indian Head he didn't know. The Constable supplied the answer.

'Funny one, all right, this. If they hadn't needed an empty over at the seed warehouse, he would have gone all the way

*

up to St Martin Station. Gypsum mill up there. They'd have
found him, I guess. Two or three days from now, maybe.
They called me and I called down to Portal and told them
we had a dead man in a Soo Line boxcar that had just come
up. Not a stitch on him, either. Whoever did it wanted his
clothes, I guess. You see some funny things if you live long
enough. Whatever happens to him now won't make much
difference.

'We would certainly appreciate your cooperation in this,'
said the man from the Consulate. 'I was instructed to request
that a set of fingerprints be sent to a, I believe, a Mister
Matthiessen in Las Vegas. The Federal Bureau of Investigation. In fact, if that could be arranged immediately, I can see
to it that the information is forwarded through Consular
channels.'

'I'm afraid I can't allow that,' said the mountie. 'Authorization would have to come through Ottawa.'

'I see,' said the man from the Consulate. 'How long do you
think that might take?'

'A day or so.'

'I was instructed to expedite the matter.'

'Sorry,' said the mountie. 'We do it by the book up here.'

'Isn't there some sort of reciprocity between police
people?'

'We like to think so,' said the mountie.

'Well, then,' said the man from the Consulate.

'You'd better talk to Ottawa,' said the mountie. 'You see
sir, I have my job to do.'

'Of course.'

'So, he'll just have to stay here for now, sir. Would you be
driving back to Winnipeg?' said the mountie. 'Because if I
were you, sir, I'd get started. It looks like nasty weather. If
you'll excuse me, sir, I'll be on my way myself now back to
District Headquarters.'

The man from the Consulate followed him outside. He
stood under a darkening sky and watched the patrol car
drive away. The Constable stood on the porch of the funeral

home. 'Guess I'll be heading home, too,' he said. 'Son of a gun, we've had some bad weather this summer.'

The funeral home was owned and operated by the man who ran the gas station, the only gas station in twenty-five miles. When the rain, the thunder and the lightning came no one was there. Two hours later, the storm had settled into a steady deluge that poured from a leaden sky – a crop spoiler the farmers would call it. The car came down the street up to its wheel-hubs in water and pulled over. It sat for several minutes with its wipers fanning the steamed windshield. Three men got out. The fourth stayed behind the wheel. When the car drove away it splattered the red mud of the northern prairies on the white gravel driveway. It dissolved into the pebbles and was gone in the mists of an early twilight.

When the car crossed the border it was nearly six o'clock and still raining. The Canadian Customs and Excise Officer wore a black slicker and a yellow plastic cover over his hat. He glanced at the card in the wallet that the man behind the wheel offered and waved the automobile through. He could not know that there was a body in the trunk of the car.

Two hours later the corpse was removed and put aboard an executive jet aircraft that stood inside a hangar at the municipal airport in Bismark, North Dakota. It was 8:22pm, Central Daylight Savings Time.

'Like I've been telling you, my family came from Havana when I was twelve years old. I don't know nothing about any of this,' said Antonio Acosta.

'How about a cigarette. Someone give him a cigarette, will you,' said the man sitting behind the desk in the small room with the soundproof door that stood wide open so that everyone could listen to everyone else and everyone could smell Antonio Acosta who smelled like fresh bread and who was still wearing his white baker's jacket and pants. When they had picked him up he had smelled even better; now the tobacco smoke was killing the rye bread.

'So what does your father do now?' said the man behind the desk.

'He lives in a wheelchair. He had a stroke,' said Acosta. 'What's this all about?'

'So that's your family life in Miami.'

'I haven't been to Miami for six years. What's this all about?'

'Speak good Cuban?' said the man behind the desk.

'Sure I speak it. What's this all about?'

'Know a lot of Cubans? They're all over the place, aren't they? Must be more than a couple of million of them. But we're interested in your friends in Miami,' said the man behind the desk. 'You know the ones I'm talking about.'

'What's this all about?'

'He wants to know what this is all about,' said the man standing in the corner of the room. 'Don't you think you ought to tell him, Fred?'

'Tell him, tell him what? He already knows,' said the man behind the desk. He looked at Acosta. 'Come on, Tony, it's all in the files so why not talk about it?'

'Talk about what?'

'The raids, Tony. The raids.'

'I was only a kid then. That was eight years ago.'

'Yeah, well we know that. No one holds it against you.'

'Then why did I spend six months in the Dade County Jail?'

'I don't know,' said the man behind the desk. 'Still feel like getting rid of Fidel?'

'Look, man, I work in a bakery in San Diego, California. I got a wife and a home. You understand? What's this all about?'

'We hear your father-in-law has some friends in Miami he stays in touch with.'

'Yeah and I wish he'd go back there. He's been living with

us for eight goddamned years. Hey – you've been out there, haven't you? You've been talking to her. You can believe about half of what she says and the other half is just noise,' said Acosta.

'That's your wife you're talking about,' said the man behind the desk.

'What's this all about?'

'Know what your father-in-law did?'

'Oh, come on now, he was a guard for some crummy outfit that paid him three bucks an hour to fall asleep on duty. So he cheated a little. Everybody in this fucking country is doing the same goddamned thing.'

'Cheated on what?'

'He wasn't supposed to be working. He got social security. Is that what this is all about?' Antonio Acosta looked at the man on the other side of the desk. 'I want to go home now, I'm tired,' he said.

'In a little while, maybe. If you'll answer the questions,' said the man.

'Any more questions and I want to see a lawyer. I know what the law is,' said Antonio Acosta.

'Sure,' said the man behind the desk. 'See what you can do about a lawyer for this boy,' he told the man standing in the corner of the room. The man nodded and walked into the other office. He sat down at an empty desk and tilted the chair far enough back so that he could put his feet up. He could hear just as well. His partner was saying: 'So you know about your father-in-law, do you? I guess he talked to you a lot, didn't he? How did he feel about Fidel?'

'What's this all about. I want a lawyer.'

From the tenth floor of the Federal Building the streets of downtown San Diego were dark. So was most of the building. Only the windows in the Field Office and the windows where the cleaning people were at work glowed in the warm night air. It was nearly 7:30pm and the city had squeezed its population back to the suburbs for the night to eat, to sleep, to love and to hate under a galaxy of stars far away and dispassionate.

The Gleason Estate was on Shoreline Drive in La Jolla. Mrs Gleason wasn't the kind of woman who liked to have her time wasted. She offered neither seats nor smiles to the two men who stood on the terra cotta floor that led from the antique oak doors into the mansion's unknown recesses.

'What is it exactly that you want?' she said. 'I can give you a couple of minutes and that's all.'

'Well, it's about your ex-husband, ma'am,' said the man with the wrinkled tie. 'We're sorry to intrude.'

'What about him?'

'Well, we'd just like to know if he's ever been in touch since — '

'Of course not,' said Mrs Gleason. 'I left Marcus Whittaker ten years ago. I haven't seen him or heard from him since.'

'Well, maybe you know something about his activities in the anti-war movement?'

'All I can remember is that he had a lot of peacenik friends up in Berkeley and that he made a fool out of himself, getting arrested and making speeches. Getting fired from the General Dynamics. There wasn't anything that Marcus wasn't capable of in those days,' said Mrs Gleason.

'We talked to some people over there. According to them it was his drinking,' said the man with the wrinkled tie.

'Oh, no. They all drink like fish. It was his silly political ideas they couldn't stand.'

'Exactly what did he do for them?'

'He designed nuclear reactors. He was quite brilliant at that, so I was told,' said Mrs Gleason. 'Now, I'm afraid you'll have to excuse me. I'm late for a charity event.'

'Could we ask you just a few more questions?'

'I'm afraid not. And, anyway, there isn't anything else I could possibly tell you,' said Mrs Gleason. She turned and walked away leaving them alone with the tapestries and the fresh flowers in the antique vases and the perfume of the night.

'Cause of death, dehydration, exposure and possibly anoxemia.' The pathologist stood in his green gown and rubber gloves back from the table and the body. The body had arrived two hours ago and he had been called in by his commanding officer. He was a Lieutenant Colonel assigned to the hospital at Nellis Air Force Base, Nevada. 'Time of death, probably about eighteen to twenty-four hours ago. A pretty healthy man, from the looks of him. Severe abrasions on wrists and ankles. Severe ecchymosis in the mastoid process. Probably caused by a blow or a fall. That's about all I can give you for now, gentlemen. Oh, and he's got ink-stained fingers.'

'Fingerprints,' said one of the agents.

'I see,' said the pathologist, 'Well, I guess that's it for now.' He stood waiting for the men to leave. The men stayed. 'If you gentlemen wish to leave — 'said the doctor.

'We'll take care of it from here,' said an agent.

'I'm not sure I understand,' said the pathologist. He looked around at the faces, started to scratch his jaw with a rubber-gloved hand, thought better of it, turned and walked through the swinging doors. An agent followed. There would be some debriefing problems ahead but nothing the Bureau couldn't handle.

'Put him back in the bag,' said the man in charge. 'Be sure and get all the pieces.'

Someone chortled. Someone retched.

A few minutes later the station wagon drove through the main gate of the base and turned toward the foxfire glow on the night's edge that was Las Vegas.

By the time they had reached their destination, the identity of the body in the back was no longer the question. A comparison of fingerprints and photographs proved that it was George Sims who had died inside the boxcar at some stage of its ninety-six hour journey from Ogden to Canada, where he had been found tied hand-and-foot under a pile of empty gunny sacks. The smart money – as the regularly assigned agents in the Las Vegas Field Office were prone to put it – was on Marcus Whittaker. The logic was simple, the conclusion obvious. The Bureau favored such constructs. Lacking evidence to the contrary they proceeded. There did remain the question of motive but that had been rather easily established: a bitter man with obviously radical connections, a knowledge of nuclear engineering and friends willing to help. It had a championship feel to it. It was something to raise the spirits of tired men.

Now, at 9:30pm, the process of tracking him down began. As always it started with the telephone calls and, as always, the results lagged well behind the true velocity of events. It was a communications lag that the Space program was accustomed to but one which the Bureau tended to misconceive. The Bureau thought like the Armed Services in this respect. An order issued was an order executed. It was the strategy of power.

'The ones you can't get on warrant, hold on suspicion,' said Howard Matthiessen, speaking to San Francisco. 'And I want surveillance – full surveillance. Of course electronic. You know the judges to call.' He hung up. He felt tired and sweaty and dirty. He punched the intercom.

'Get that fellow from the nuclear safeguards office over here. You know the one, the Japanese,' he said. 'And arrange to have my suitcase brought over.'

At least things were taking on a predictable shape, he thought. That was what Washington would want to hear.

This Whittaker, whoever he was, was no dope. It had the feel of politics in it. And, maybe, some extortion, though of what kind remained to be seen. Calls to newspapers and the media. A fantasy of public approval. National attention. If that happened, the cat was out of the bag. That, decided Matthiessen, could not be allowed to happen. Under any circumstances.

Five minutes later, in a clean suit, shirt, underwear, socks and tie, he was issuing his instructions.

'Every newspaper, television and radio station in the region will be notified that any calls or messages relating to the matter at hand must be reported immediately and that we request their co-operation in keeping this under wraps until the situation is resolved. Use the stolen drugs cover.'

'But they'll know won't they?' said someone. 'I mean they'll know what was really taken.'

'No basis in fact,' said Matthiessen. 'If we have to or if it comes to that we'll produce denials from the highest sources. Any other questions?'

There was one: 'The railroad people. What are we going to do about them?'

'I think it's been pretty well contained. Just the management echelons and the security people,' said Matthiessen. 'Seems to me there was one of them who was giving them trouble. Check on that with the man we left up there, Morse, I think it is. Tell him to make sure that whoever it is keeps his mouth shut. Seems to me, he was one of their Yard security people.

'Maybe we should pull him in,' said someone.

'Not unless it becomes necessary,' said Matthiessen. 'We want co-operation, not confussion. At least not until we know how it happened.'

'This Whittaker,' said someone. 'He could be some kind of psycho. They usually are.'

'It's up to you gentlemen to find out,' said Matthiessen. 'And to find him.'

They left the office, just a small group of men who knew their job. It gave Howard Matthiessen a sense of pleasure and pride to know that the organization was in high gear. That was what the Bureau was all about.

The telephone buzzed. He picked it up.

'Mister Shigata to see you, sir,' said the voice.

'I'll be with him in a few minutes,' said Matthiessen. 'Get me Washington.'

He looked out through the window at Las Vegas. It was the kind of place he despised. A city without honor, purpose or meaning, a marketplace for cheap temptations – sin, flesh and the devil. He preferred the vices of arrogance, power and politics, the stuff of History. Perhaps the man they were looking for did, too, wherever he was.

The call for Joe Morse dangled in electronic limbo for five minutes while the receptionist at the Ogden Operations Center tried to locate him. She failed and took the message from the man at the other end. She put the switchboard on hold, paid a brief visit to the ladies room, and took it upstairs. The fourth floor was deserted except for somebody from the mail room pushing his cart down the hall. He looked old and tired and he moved slowly. She nodded and he shrugged. She put the message on Joe's borrowed desk and went home for the night.

Chapter Eleven

It was 10:30pm and Mulloy was on his way to Mexico. He had missed Slim at Grand Junction and he had missed him at Pueblo and he had missed him by two hours at Santa Fe, New Mexico. Now, the freight he was riding was south of Tucson and headed for the border where he would probably miss him again. The old man had slipped away from him each time because he was running as scared and fast as he could. Mulloy had found that out from another drifter who he had rousted out of a lean-to in the hobo jungle on the edge of the Santa Fe yard. According to the drifter, Slim had been there – and so had another fellow who was looking for him – who was in just as much of a big hurry as Slim.

'What kind of fellow?' Mulloy had asked.

'Oh,' said the drifter, 'Big. He was a real big one. Young, too. Had a crazy look about him, I think.'

Mulloy sat in the caboose watching the night slide by and listening to the cheerful voice of the train conductor. He was dog-tired and his bones ached. He felt like an old elephant on its way to a graveyard where it would trumpet once and slide into oblivion. But the conductor wouldn't let him.

'This state's got lots of trouble because of the people who moved here,' said the conductor. 'They came in here to grab, just like the old days. Everybody grabbing everything. Sooner or later I guess that's got to end. If you stand up and say so nobody's going to listen to you. It's all falling apart, if you ask me.'

Mulloy thought he must mean society but he wasn't listening. He had wandered off again into instant replays of his life. There were no cheering crowds. The stadium was dark and empty.

There was a nudie calendar girl tacked to the wall. Raped by a thousand eyes but still smiling through the fly-specks. 'How long before we get into Nogales?'

'See out there – all them cars on the highway. That's where they're headed, too. We'll beat them. You going across the border?'

'Maybe.'

'Well, you'll have to walk but it's only ten feet between them and us. You got business down there?'

'Yeah. Some things.'

'Something missing, is it?'

'Something,' said Mulloy. It was human cargo he was looking for – not transistor radios. It was an old man. Flotsam from the wreckage of the country that had sunk. Old Slim, the last coyote on the raft.

'There ought to be a zoo,' Mulloy said.

'We got a zoo. A good zoo in Tucson . . . what for?' said the conductor.

'For people who don't fit in this world anymore.'

'We got a good museum, too. Full of dinosaur and Indian stuff,' he said. 'We're coming in now.'

The air was spicy and hot. It was the smell of Mexico. Mulloy walked up from the back of the train and found a man in the security office he used to know from a long time ago when the guy worked in Barstow.

'What you doing down here? You must have come down on the wetback special.'

'Looking for an easy rider.'

'Lots of them around here.'

'One of the old timers.'

'Not so many of those. We got more progressive types using the facilities. Lose about one or two a week.'

'What from?'

'Overdose of knife blade. For the money they might be taking back down; the money they earned from sneaking in here to work the grapefruits or whatever else needs picking, weeding and a miserable son of a bitch to do it.'

'That's what I'm afraid of.'

'You ought to talk to the Immigration boys. They're the ones that usually pick up the pieces.'

'His name's Slim.'

'That old son of a gun? I'll be damned. What's he up to?'

'Nothing. There was a little trouble up the line. I'm just checking it out.'

'Well, I can tell you where you'll find him.'

'How's that?'

'Up with the Indians. He's got himself a place outside of Magdalena. Where what's left of them hang around, or live, or whatever they do. Not like the troublemakers we got in Arizona. Not that they don't have their rights but they got no right to hold back the water project. That's the way I see it, anyway.'

'Any trains going down that way?'

'The same one you came in on. Leaves in about half an hour.'

'Thank you kindly.'

'How's it going up in Ogden? I heard there was some trouble over a boxcar. Government stuff. You involved in that?'

'Not me. I'm just a dumb yardbull.'

'That's one hard-nosed railroad you're working for. If you ever get fed up come down and talk to me. I know some people up in Phoenix and we might be able to fix it up.'

'I'll keep it in mind,' said Mulloy.

'You do that,' the old guy replied. Mulloy felt gratified to know that his work was so appreciated. 'We need a good man now and then.'

'You don't know my bad side,' Mulloy replied.

'That's your secret,' he said, rubbing his tired, red eyes.

Out in the Yard they were moving boxcars around – the old way. Gangs of men and a lot of shouting back and forth in a mixture of Spanish and cussing. A hot, night wind was blowing up from the Sonora – the Coronado they called it, the ill wind from the south.

Mulloy climbed aboard the caboose and stared at the lady on the wall again. Fired, broke, finished, he was on his way to Mexico. What the hell was he doing, he wondered, searching for the fountain of youth? That wasn't Coronado, that was someone else. He never found it. Life aboard the crummies, one caboose after another, always at the ass end of the gut. Ticket good for life, nailed to your hand by the bad luck of all the generations that came before thee, the poor potato farmers and the dumb immigrants and the ignorant and the lecherous and the conniving. All of them, with all of their anger, their bitterness, their meaningless resentment of everything including existence, itself. Sitting on barstools, carriers of the disease of consciousness. Always moving on the curl of the wave that smashed. The self-pity was sweet and delicious. He needed a drink but Charley's bottle had been finished long ago.

A big young brute in a conductor's uniform climbed aboard. They moved, jounced and swayed away from the neon and the glare out into the dark desert sea and Mulloy was thinking of Pearl and wondering if they would tow away her car and whether he was tired enough to hit one of the stinky bunks in the front and whether he should take a couple of pills for the headache and the general ache of everything when he raised his eyes and the son of a bitch had his gun on him.

'Keep your hands on the table, brother,' he said.

They sat and looked at each other. The kid had milky eyes and a half-smile on his all-American boy's face. He was at least six-two, probably taller. Except for one thing, he looked like the fullback on the high-school football team.

'You've got bad teeth,' said Mulloy.

He tapped the butt of the gun on the knuckles of Mulloy's left hand. It hurt. He said, 'Stand up, brother.' Mulloy stood. They moved out into the aisle. He said, 'Lie down, brother.' Mulloy lay down. The kid wired his wrists together with a length of wire from his pocket. He said, 'Get up, brother.' Mulloy managed to do it. They sat down again. He said, 'We'll have to wait for a spell before I take care of you.' He took out a package of gumdrops, of all things, and popped a handful one after another into his mouth. His coach wouldn't have liked that.

'Cigarette — ?' said Mulloy.

'It's a filthy, dirty habit, brother,' he said.

'So is gobbling your food.'

He put down the gumdrops and open-handed Mulloy on the side of the head. It hurt. The kid sat back and smiled in a soft, self-satisfied way. He picked up his gumdrop count. He was a real lulu. Where all other emotions fail, fear succeeds. If this was the guy Mulloy thought he was, there was a good reason for the hollow feeling in the stomach and the twitch at the corner of the mouth that wouldn't stop. If this was the guy then it was just Mulloy's bad luck. But maybe he was just a loony. Just a kid with a problem. Drugs. Something. Whatever. The straws of that idea all blew away and the time passed. Mulloy looked at the calendar lady. His eyes followed. He reached across the aisle and ripped her down and crumpled her up. He gave Mulloy that smile. He ate his last gumdrop, yawned, leveled the gun at him and said, 'You get up now and do like you're told and you won't get hurt no more. Just move out the back door.' He reached around and opened it. Mulloy didn't want to get hurt no more so he did like he was told.

The night was pitch black and they were moving right along – maybe forty, maybe fifty miles an hour on bad tracks, the kind that sway you and bounce you in all directions at once. Mulloy stood with his feet apart and braced himself against the guard rail. The kid was behind him. The air was full of dryness and leftover heat. The desert was discharging the fury of the day. Mulloy knew he was about to get clobbered and then flung into that swirling space, perhaps to fall forever. It was that strange moment of knowing.

'Move over there, brother,' said the kid.

For reasons that will remain forever obscure Mulloy gave him a kick in the general direction of the petunias, the recalcitrant mule kick. It missed and the kid lashed out, and pushed and Mulloy lost his balance and grabbed at something – the kid's belt and they went over the side together. The belt broke and Mulloy was rolling head over heels bouncing on jello, all numbed-out. And then it was still.

Mulloy crawled a little way, then got up and ran and tripped and fell and got up and ran again for as long as he could, as far as he could until his lungs wouldn't push his body any farther. The darkness had endless dangerous depths and now he was afraid again, like a blindfolded child with one foot on what his friends told him was the edge of something awful. If the kid came at him now, Mulloy was finished. He found a boulder and put his back against it and floated away.

When he came back there was something he had to do. He worked on the wire and rested and worked on the wire until his wrists were a bloody mess. The sky tinged pink in the East and he was still working. A full glow spread across the horizon. There was a jagged edge on the rock and he hooked his bleeding wrists round it, got up on his knees and pulled against the rawness and the nausea. The wire came apart and he lay face down in the dirt all ripped and broken but free.

And the gun was there, strapped up against his armpit, the wonderful Smith and Wesson with six big fat ones that he wasn't about to waste. He was the primal man with his club, a real Neanderthal. It took five minutes to get out of his shirt and ten more to rip it up. He wrapped the bandages around his wrists and managed to tie a couple of loose knots with the fingers that worked. A couple of them didn't. There was blood all over everything and the sun was coming up. Another few years and he would have gone over the edge of a canyon. It was dark and deep and on the other side of the cliffs rose in terraces of eroded loins of sandstone glowing pink in the morning light. To one side there were cliffs, too. The gullies and the boulders and the ravines blocked him off from the railroad tracks but they would be over there where the sun was climbing into the cloudless sky. When the kid came as Mulloy knew he would, he wanted to be above him. So he started to climb. A few yards and he knew it was no good. The sandstone was rotten and his hands were no help at all. He realized that he could stay where he was or go down. Maybe he could get to the bottom and maybe he would get stuck. If he reached the bottom maybe there would be an easy way out. Maybe there wouldn't. If he stayed where he was he would have to shoot the kid up close. His hands could barely hold the gun. He didn't think the kid would try to get that close. Mulloy decided to go down. If he wanted to follow that was fine with him. Nail him as he came. That would be enjoyable. Mulloy was thinking like a wounded animal, like you thought on the battlefield after a mine or a mortar had shellacked you good, leaving you dazed and bloody and not giving a damn, anymore.

Something splattered against the rock. It was a spent bullet. The sound of the gun caught up. There he was six or seven hundred yards away, shooting at the moon. He was moving up the hill that led to the edge of the canyon and taking his time about it. There was no hurry. There was no thrill. It was just a morning's work.

For Mulloy the climbing idea was out. The present position was untenable, too. There was one direction to move and that was along the side of the steep slope behind him. It was not going to be easy going. If he wants me that bad, he thought, he would have to follow, the son of a bitch.

Mulloy crawled around the rock and used it for a shield, then stood up and moved off. His legs felt disjointed and weak and the bad knee was loose. If it went out, that would be all she wrote. Korea would finally catch up, the slow acting poison of events. It was something to think about moving across the crumbly sand that rose steeply toward the breast of the first overhang. The kid took another crack at him and it was way off. Mulloy wondered if he had extra rounds because he had used two already.

The side of the hill folded around the cliff and when Mulloy was there he looked back and the kid was still coming. The sun was high now, and he decided not to think about what it was going to be like in an hour, or in three hours, or even longer. There was only one thing to worry about and that was the cliffs. They had to be approached with enthusiasm and confidence. They had to be understood and loved, like the noble mountaineers pretended when they were hanging on a bunch of ropes drinking Budweiser beer.

This was just a castle of sand stuck together in the middle of nowhere with a layer of this and a layer of that running across it in wide, horizontal bands. No big deal. And he was the playboy of the western world, the fearless Mulloy, watch him, ladies and gentlemen, as he becomes the human fly.

He took another goddamn shot. It was closer. The kid was closer. Right in front of Mulloy's feet there was a nice, wide ledge and he walked out on it and pretended that it wouldn't let him down. When it did, he wasn't stunned and amazed. That was how things were. The ledge just ended.

Mulloy didn't want to look down so he looked up. There was a nice strong mesquite bush growing sideways out of a hole in the rock. It invited him to have a try. It said, *just reach out, stand on your toes, and give a little leap. I promise all things to all believers.*

Mulloy took the leap and hung, legs dangling out in space and then scrabbling for something to cling to. They found it and he levered himself up and the whole thing was easy. There was another ledge above the bush and he made that too. There was a small, spotted lizard on the ledge and it looked at him, flickered and was gone. The ledge was a dead end in both directions.

Mulloy went up. From bush to crack to foothold to terrible moment where there was nothing to scratch and claw at except smooth, treacherous rock. He went up and up and up and the wind decided to blow, little gusts that got stronger and bigger whipping at him from one direction, then another, filling his eyes with grit, insulting the wonderful purity and integrity of the experience. He went up until there was nothing above him but a little chimney pipe cut deep in the sandstone. It looked easy and it was easy and he almost lost it half-way when a chunk of it broke off under his foot, leaving him bent double like a fetus clinging to the side of the womb with nothing below but the sheer emptiness of the depths of the world. A few more feet and he was there.

On top. The wind blasted at him and tried to push him back. He crawled away from the edge wanting to rest. But he knew he had to keep going. His little journey had taken him to the top of a promontory that stuck out from the main wall of the gorge and pitched up to join it in a succession of steep little knobs.

Going up the knobs was as bad as climbing sand dunes. He took them one-by-one. He was about half-way to the top and taking a blow when the kid arrived. He'd found the better way. He had come around the point and climbed up the other side. From where Mulloy stood he could see that it was practically a walk. They were a thousand yards apart. Mulloy waved at him. The kid waved back and Mulloy gave him the finger. He started coming and Mulloy started going. It was an inexorable relationship. The wind blew and the sun beat on him and each leg was full of lead.

The last one was the worst. Of course. Loose and steep. Mulloy crawled up to the place where the remaining forty feet were straight up again. Juniper roots had laced their way down from the rim. It was a beanstalk and he started to climb it. Then there was a whang and a splat and then another just about where his foot had been. Mulloy craned his neck around and saw the kid. He was about fifty yards downhill, spread-eagled and bracing the gun with both hands. Mulloy wrapped an arm around the thick root, clawed at his holster, found the goddamned thing, hung there and aimed it in his general direction and let one loose. It kicked up the sand in front of the kid who hightailed it across the side of the hill and disappeared. Mulloy couldn't get the gun back where it belonged so he shoved it down his belt where it got all tangled up in underwear and pubic hair. Giving the kid a taste of it was what Mulloy had needed. The feeling pulled him up the rest of the way to the top.

Mulloy lay on his stomach for a while looking down. Nothing moved. He got up and looked the other way and it was rugged country, a jumble of rock and brush and dry washes that led off toward more of the same and ended where the next set of ridges poked at the immensity of cloudless sky. Airplanes flew over it at thirty-thousand feet and it looked like nothing. Passengers slept and woke up feeling groggy in an air-conditioned terminal with tinted windows and the smell of deodorized people moving from one super-dome to another soothed by the musak, full of indifference. He was very thirsty and very tired and the nearest free champagne was up there somewhere but he couldn't see it because the light was burning sharp, snapping at the edges of his vision.

He had to find a place, a rock or a tree or a hole in the ground, something to crawl into and with a view. A room with a view. It was that or go after the kid. Go after him and get it over with one way or another. The feeling came to Mulloy that he wasn't going to make it. He was too tired and old and confused and not hard enough anymore, lie down and curl up and sleep, little baby, said the feeling. Suck your thumb and drift away. No more worries forever. Fading away on billowing waves of warm, green water. Sinking into the blessed depths.

It was the gun that pulled him back. The front sight was gouging him in the crotch and the pain woke him up. He was lying on his stomach with his mouth full of sand. Maybe five minutes had passed. He was up and moving on sore feet and stiffening legs, taking the easy way – up the flat middle of a dry wash that meandered off through the boulders and the brush. The kid would track him easy and Mulloy didn't care. He was looking for his hole in the ground.

He had almost found it when the kid almost got him.

Mulloy might have come a mile up the dead creek. It had narrowed down and walls of rock were forming on either side. The wind was howling right straight in his face and he didn't see or hear anything until the bullet smashed up a rock about two feet from his head. He hit the dirt and tried to roll behind something and tried to get his own piece. His eyes roved around and spotted the kid, about forty, fifty yards away leaning up against an outcropping, with the revolver down at his side. The Sunday stroller out for a walk in the Sonora desert. Jolly good fellow. Mulloy took another

pop at him. It was way off to the left. The kid faded behind
his rock and Mulloy took off. Up the funnel. It broadened
out again into a thicket of dead cottonwood and tumbleweed. Going through it was like forcing his way through
barbed wire. Where it finished things got worse. The gulley
ended in a pile of twisted rock that flood waters had ejected.
It went up and up and up and he knew he wasn't going to
climb it. Not today. Only far enough to look back down.

He was about there when the kid took his last shot at him.
Another throw-away from off to the left and there he was,
the insane, demented asshole oversized kid with rotten teeth
who didn't like dirty pictures on the wall, even in appropriate
places. There he was with a big grin pasted on his face holding up the gun and showing Mulloy it was empty. The kid
tossed it away and just stood there smirking. Mulloy sat on a
hot flat piece of rock and looked down at him. You mother-
fucker, he thought. You loony son of a bitch.

'Hey!' Mulloy yelled. 'I'm going to waste you. I'm going to
do it.'

And make the world a better place.

'I'm a law officer. You can give yourself up!' said Mulloy.

It was hilarious. The wind blew for a while. There was
nothing but the two of them. Start the teargas, boys, and then
move in behind the flak-proof vests. Tell all the reporters
to stay behind the armored cars and don't use your flame
throwers indiscriminately. Might get the neighbors upset.
When he comes out riddle him with dum-dum bullets and tell
the world there was no other way.

Mulloy couldn't get off the hook. But he took it out, himself.

The kid pulled a something out of his pocket, undid it,
bent down, found a nice round rock, and, in a blur of quick-
ness, delicacy, speed and accuracy such as one sees rarely
except on TV, unleashed it at Mulloy with the sound of whip
crack. It was a sling. Right out of David and Goliath. That
was what the guy had and he knew how to use it. Mulloy
ducked and the missile sailed past his ear and ricocheted
into the small of his back. By the time he got the gun up

he was gone. All Mulloy wanted was a couple of cracks at him. He felt he was going to go down soon. Body knowledge. That was what was going to happen. The creep out there – where did he get all his energy? Out there in the shimmering, flowing, mystical universe of rock surrounded by the red mists that were sinking over everything.

The next one hit Mulloy in the right forearm and broke it. Nice-looking, ordinary rock. It was broken all right and white-hot spasms shot up through the elbow all the way to the neck. Nice looking, ordinary rock. Couldn't use the gun, not anymore. Couldn't use anything. Didn't know what to do. There he was, the kid coming. Working his way through the brush. He is coming up to bash my head in now, thought Mulloy. Big rock to bash in the head.

There was a big ball of skeleton-dry greasewood close enough to reach. Lit a match and it blew out. Lit the book and shoved it in the tangle. The thing went up like a phosphorus bomb. Kicked it over the edge. Watched it bounce and bound until it reached the bottom. It hit a dead tree and the tree went up like it was full of flash powder. It hit another tumbleweed and it went up. The wind pushed and the flames roared. The kid saw what was happening and tried his damnedest to get the hell out of there. Instead, he got hung up on a tree limb. The fire just ate him up like meat on a skewer. Mulloy didn't look at what was left of him.

A long time passed and the fire was gone and Mulloy was walking across the hot ashes and he was there and he didn't look then, either. He is probably still there, thought Mulloy, walking and falling and crawling across the surface of the moon, trying to get back home. Home in the arms of the earth.

In the dream he was being tossed up and down on a trampoline by a bunch of circus clowns. Each time he hit they said, 'Madre Dios!' and he woke up and asked them who he was and they said *'Quien sabe, olvidado?'*, *who knows, lost one?* And in the dream time ran in spirals and something horrible chased him through the black night to the cliff, a giggling slavering thing as tall as a house with blood dripping from its fangs howling and shrieking and growling wanting to devour his soul. He threw a rock at it and it changed into a pillar of fire, a whirlwind of flames roaring away across the desert hissing and screaming vengeance at the Universe. In the dream people came out of the shadows at him, the old man with his exaggerated brogue telling him to go to sleep and not waiting before love was made on worn out, bouncing hotel bedsprings, stale air and boozy breathing, the sorrowful rustle of money changing hands. His father, user of women, forgive him if you can. And himself for his transgressions of emotion, the twisting and turning of the heart away from what was real until nothing was. The days of betrayal are the worst, filling you with the bitterness and the loss. In the dream Pearl was saying, 'I'll never be who you think I am or what you want me to be,' as she lay on the bed legs spread wide apart, coupling with one, then another and another and they were all the man from Denver who took her away in the big car to make her into a proper whore which was what she wanted and knowing never changes anything. We are what we are, ever searching for what we are not. Twenty years of it. Just a dumb kid with his heart in his hand. Not so dumb anymore.

Mulloy woke up when they dumped him off the back of the truck seeing the shadows that laced the brown. Someone was holding his head, giving him water, smelling of garlic and armpits. It was a son of the church, and that was what they were for. The water trickled down his chin. He drifted away hearing the toll of the bell, one clear note hanging on the hard air summoning him into darkness again.

Chapter Twelve

The two-lane highway and the railroad tracks unraveled out of the Needle Mountains side-by-side, a ribbon of tar and a ribbon of steel winding down from the hard, cold edges of the world through streaks of ancient lava, glittering rock and anomalous dust, the colors of it all sucked away by the thirsty sun leaving nothing but ashes.

The car and the freight came down together: first the freight and then the car, shuffling the lead back and forth until the road straightened and schussed directly down into the ochres and afternoon purples of the desert. Then the car pulled ahead leaving the train far behind. The train was a short haul freight coming over from Modena with mine scratchings and mostly empty ore carriers, rusted and sun-battered, too old for the main line and not worth fixing. The boxcar riding at the tail-end stood out in striking contrast. It was new and it was a Chesapeake and Ohio, moved by some strange alchemy of events all the way from the East Coast to the far shores of the Rockies on a migration that no natural-ist would understand and one that even the custodian of the waybills sitting up front with the engineer and the trainmen found puzzling. Consigned to 567 until notified, said the waybill. 567 was the siding at Dempster, Dempster's Disaster, as it was known to the locals – the great uranium find of '51 – the seam of carnotite that would be so rich in megatons that the world need look no further than this little corner of the Utah desert for its nuclear fires. The mine had been a bust. A lot of Eastern investors had gone broke and so had Jim Dempster. He still lived in La Vern and his mine was still out there about twenty-five miles from town. Why the hell anyone would want to dump a boxcar out there the train conductor didn't know. His job was to deliver it, or see that it was delivered. From the engine cab window he saw the car passing them going down the long grade that led into La Vern. It was nothing special, except for the Government plates. It kicked up a tail of dust and sped toward the distant town. They would be there themselves in a half-hour. It was 3:45 in the afternoon already and they had to turn around and go back.

Joe Morse parked the car on the diagonal in front of the red brick Victorian building with the copper cupola. He tried to feed a dime to the parking meter but it was broken. There were four or five pick-ups down the street and three or four people. There was a Tabernacle and a hardware store, the Virtues by which the Mormons were supposed to live. It was a dry county and this was the seat. The congregation of the bottle club would far outnumber the faithful. The thought brought a sneaky sense of satisfaction. He got out of the car and, full of such heresies, climbed the worn stone steps and went through the squeaky oak door into the shade of the Town Offices.

There was one grey-haired lady behind a manual typewriter and two men in white shirts with the sleeves rolled up. One of them wore a badge. They had the fat look of people who did practically nothing.

'I'd like to look at some of your land records,' he told the woman. 'Deeds and conveyances, that sort of thing.'

'Yessir,' said the one with the badge. 'What can we do for you?'

'He's already said what he wanted,' said the lady. 'He wants to go through the land files.'

The man looked at his watch. 'I guess you've got about a half-hour,' he said. 'We close up.' The sentence dangled in the musty, dry air.

It didn't take him that long, although he found nothing at

all. No records of purchase or conveyance that had George Jarvis's name on it – none within the last two and a half years. In fact, not very much in the way of transactions involving anyone at all. It was a little too bizarre, anyway, the whole idea. On the previous evening, he should have exercised his normal quota of skepticism toward the lady who was coming down the steps of the dilapidated turn-of-the-century house as he followed the brick path through the weed-filled yard.

It had been close to eleven o'clock and the sound of crickets filled the night. She was wearing a black warm-up suit with florescent stripes taped around each leg in spirals like barbers' poles. Her white hair was rolled around big, pink curlers and she looked about eighty years old. Joe Morse had introduced himself.

'You got to wait until I do my two miles,' she said.

'I'm in a hurry, too,' said Joe.

'Well — ' she said. 'Out with it, then.'

'One of your roomers. Mister Jarvis.'

'Are you a policeman?'

'I'm with the Federal Bureau of Investigation.'

'What are you snooping around here for?'

'I'm not snooping, ma'am. I just want to know if a Mister Jarvis lives at this address.'

'He did. Why aren't you home in bed like the rest of the world?' Her eyes made quick, shrewd appraisals.

'Well, I would be but I had to come down here,' said Joe. 'You see, Mister Jarvis might be in some trouble.'

'I wouldn't be surprised the way he was carrying on,' she said.

'He's not living here now?'

'Moved out a week ago. One bag. Just the way he came. Never even said goodbye. Not that I expected it.'

'Carrying on — ?' Joe said, picking up the titbit that she had dropped dead-center on the target like an old seagull wise in the ways of unprotected heads.

'That's what I said. Carrying on. Yelling, screaming and hollering half the night about this, that and the other thing. Nothing but a damn fool could be bothered.'

'About what?'

'Whether he was going to get to heaven or hell,' she said. 'Stick around, I'll be back.' She charged by him down the path jumped out through the gate. Under the street lights, the stripes jumped up and down and winked away into the night. Joe sat and waited. He stared at the worn-out crepe soles of his shoes and listened to the flurry and stir of the August insects. Such lullabyes had vanished from his own life with time and the passage of the years and there was a lot to regret in that and no way of changing it.

The old marathon runner came back. She charged up the steps past Joe, yelled, 'I'll be right back,' and the screen door slammed behind her. She came back out wearing levis and cowboy boots. She looked like a healthy scarecrow. 'You got five minutes before I watch my television program. Then you're on your way.'

'Do you know why he left?' asked Joe.

'Mister Jarvis, you mean?'

'That's who I mean.'

'Sure I know why he left. It was that church of his – the whole damned lot of them. Getting ready for Judgment Day. You never saw anything like it.'

'Like what?'

'The praying and the hollering. If you want to know the truth of it, I was ready to kick him out anyway. He was upsetting the other tenants.'

'Any idea where he might have gone?'

'Sure. Down there in the desert. They called it the promised land. Him and his wives.'

'Wives — ?'

'That's what I said. He was nothing but one of them polygamists. That's against the law. Against nature, too. I was married for thirty-six years. One of me was enough.'

'How many wives did he have?'

'How should I know? They'd come and they'd go. Some

was young and some was old. Spent their time ringing door-bells all around town handing out tracts. Like them Jehovahs do.'

'Got any idea what part of the desert?'

'Sure. Down south in some godforsaken place. That's where his mail came from.'

'That's a big help,' said Joe.

'It's time for my program,' said the old lady.

He was half-way down the path when she yelled at him, 'No children. Ain't none of them had any. Had four, myself. Maybe they was all too busy getting to heaven to have any time for *that*.' The screen door slammed and the television set went on.

He was half-way down the path when she yelled at him again, 'Forgot something.' She came outside. She was gnaw-ing on a chicken leg. She waved it at him. 'He's got a sister living over in Brigham City somewhere. She come down here one time tried to talk him into giving it up. Threw her right out. A poor little nothing of a woman. Married to some fellow up there. Stokes, that was her name.' The chicken leg delivered a final flourish. The television set said, 'And here's Johnny.'

Joe had then driven to Brigham City. It took him three hours to find Rachel Stokes. When he banged on the door of the drab and dark little farm house with no telephone and no electricity it took five minutes before it opened and another ten to soothe the bearded man with the shotgun and the flashlight who stood inside and told him to go away before he got his head blown off. It took another hour to get Rachel to talk about George Jarvis, her brother, and then all she would say in a dulled and stupefied voice was that he had fled from the sight of God and that he would surely burn in hell for his sins and heresies.

Her husband sat with his shotgun across his knees in the lantern light and a baby squalled from somewhere upstairs. She got up and left. The room had newspapers tacked over the windows instead of curtains. The man, Stokes, just sat.

They were the desolated and the God-driven, stunted and desiccated, the withered seed of Abraham, begetter of nations, the inheritors of a scorching wind.

'Here, brother,' said the husband. He produced a tattered envelope. It was a letter from George Jarvis. The contents were missing. The return address was La Vern, Utah. 'They live there on land bought from the devil. You better git, now.'

Whoever owned the land bought from the devil it wasn't Jarvis. He closed the worn-out old ledger and walked down the hall to the front office. The men were gone and the woman was putting the cover over her typewriter. She had never heard of anyone by that name. 'Try Jim Dempster,' she said. 'He knows most everything that goes on around here.'

'Where do I find him?'

'The McBride Home for the Aged. Down that way. Now, wait a minute, it's time for the train. He'll meet that. Always does. Try over there at the station. You can hear it coming now.' The town shook under the rumble and the roar.

The old man with the yellowed-white hair wore gabardine trousers a size too big and wide, red suspenders to hold them up. Under them was a plaid skirt with a can of Bull Durham tobacco in the pocket and a string tie with a tarnished clasp. He climbed stiffly up into the cab of the diesel locomotive and sat down in the brakeman's seat. The engineer said, 'How you feeling today, Jim?'

'Not too good, not too bad,' said Jim Dempster. 'Not much of a load today.'

'We're ready when you are.'

'I'm always ready. All I need is a little of somebody else's money. Give me that and I could take a hundred tons a day out of there.'

'I'll bet you could, too,' said the engineer.

'You got a boxcar back there,' said Jim. 'Second one in three days to the same place. Couple of others up there already, too.'

'It's going out to your siding by the mine,' said the engineer. 'If the damn switch engine's running. What you got in there, a bunch of fancy women?'

'It's them fellows renting my warehouse.'

'What are they doing way to hell and gone up there?'

'Didn't ask and they didn't say.'

'Maybe they're stealing your uranium,' said the engineer.

'Did I ever tell you about the time I was invited to that opera house of theirs in New York City,' said Jim, ignoring the sally. 'Had to buy myself a long-tailed suit.'

'You mean the Grand Old Oprey,' said the engineer.

'Hell, no. I mean the *real* old oprey,' said Jim.

'That must have been something.'

'It was something,' said Jim.

'Excuse me,' said the engineer. He stuck his head out the side window. 'Looks like we're ready to move. You take care of yourself, hear.'

'No way I wouldn't,' said Jim Dempster, climbing down.

The locomotive moved off. A man threw a switch and it came back along the other track and hooked up to the far end of the haul. The crew climbed up and the train moved off. The old yard engine roared like a sick mule and moved past Jim going in the other direction, pushing the boxcar out front. The man inside waved and Jim waved back. The town was asleep again.

The man that came up to him had a pleasant face, a suit that needed pressing and a tired voice.

'They said you might be able to help me,' he said. 'The name is Morse.' They shook.

'Can't say whether I can or I can't,' said Jim.

'I'm looking for a fellow name of Jarvis. Thought you might have heard of him.'

'Nope,' said Jim.

'There might be some people he's associated with. A church group. They might own some land around here.'

'Plenty of that kind,' said Jim.

'Well, they might be a little bit different than your run of the mill.'

'Plenty of them, too,' said Jim.

'Wherever it is, it's called the Promised Land.'

'I know them,' said Jim. 'You could hardly miss them.'

'Is that so?'

'Live like a pack of wolves out there. So I hear.'

'How would I find them?'

'Up toward Indian Peak. Not much in the way of roads.'

'Maybe you could draw me a map,' said Morse.

'It's rough country.'

'How about a cup of coffee?'

'If you've got the money, I've got the time. Plenty of that,' said Jim Dempster.

'Anywhere I can make a phone call?' said Joe Morse. He looked down the empty railroad tracks, the shimmer of steel in hot light, the stretching out of space and time, the line drawn between earth and sky. 'Then we'll sit down and you can draw me a map,' he said. It was as simple as that.

The Chesapeake and Ohio boxcar stood on the rusted track and refused to move. The diesel switch engine that had pushed it up to the mine had backed off. It came forward again slowly and gave a shove. The engineer leaned out of the cab and watched it roll forward a few yards and stop again. He peered at the rails and at the switch beyond. God-damn them, anyway, sending things up here, he thought. And it was getting late, too. He revved up, moved up and gave her a real whack in the ass. She shot across the frozen switch and rolled down the gentle grade that led to what was left of Dempster's ore-crushing mill. He could see the end of another car down there sticking out from behind the side of the building. 'Sorry about that,' he said. He pulled the whistle cord, filling the air with a chorus of eerie and derisive hoots, and headed for town.

The shadow of the boxcar moved across the piles of old machinery and along the side of the sand-blasted buildings that leaned away from the north wind. Wheels squeaked and a loose bearing rattled. With a loud bang, it hit and the other cars crashed against each other. There was the creak of cooling steel and then silence. Far away to the west the light was red-tongued, licking the bones of the mountains. The sky was liquid purple, a bottomless vat of ancient wine. Jupiter glittered already, rising low in the East.

'The crowbar,' said the Angel of Death.

He used the crowbar. The doors slid back with the sound of thunder. Then it was silent again.

The cross was carved into the side of a cliff. The old man in town had told Joe Morse about that but it was still quite a sight with the last rays of the sun etching it out of the shadows. Someone had gone to a lot of trouble and risk to climb up there and to chip out fifty feet of granite. Some nut, thought Joe. Someone with nothing better to do. The car lurched sideways. A tire blew with a bang and he was thrown against the steering wheel. There was a hissing noise and the radiator erupted in gouts of brown boiling water. He slammed the brakes and stopped. The temperature warning light was on. He killed the engine and got out. The rock that had done the trick was right in the middle of the dirt track and he had driven right over it because he had been looking up instead of down.

The radiator hissed for another five minutes and then it stopped. The air was turning cold and the twilight was almost gone. What the hell, he thought. Whatever's up in there can't be much further. Maybe they can give me some help. He followed the fresh tire tracks that marked the crude road. The earth was warm and the spice of the desert was dry and pungent. It felt good to move his legs after all the hours in the car. In his imagination he was young again, full with the end of the day, the last miles of a hard journey. The illusion soon passed. He trudged on.

The tracks twisted toward the cliffs. The air had a biting edge now, and the sky was black and fertile with stars. God's grandeur, thought Joe Morse, moving into oblivion.

Chapter Thirteen

'Let me tell you something,' said Fernando, hider of wet-backs. 'There ain't no son of a bitch in this whole, stinking wide world going to lay a finger on you. Got me?'

Slim nodded his head slowly and scratched a flea bite on his chest. He had another drink of whatever it was he was drinking having forgotten what it was because whatever it was had made him drunk and being drunk felt good because it made him feel mean as a mule and strong as a horse and filled his veins with the fires of youth.

'You don't believe me, that I mean what I say,' said Fernando, red-rimmed eyes glistening in the light of the hurricane lantern hung on the beam of the shack. 'Didn't I take you back across the border, didn't I get you here, old man?'

'Tin Can City,' said Slim. 'Hiding in the back of a truck just like a wetback. You got me to Tin Can City and it cost me a hundred bucks.'

'What's a hundred bucks? It means nothing,' said Fernando. 'It was a favor. If you got more money, I wouldn't take none of it. You got more money, old man?'

'Not on me,' said Slim.

'Maybe you want to go to work for me. Easy work in the lettuce fields. Make a lot of money.'

'Nope,' said Slim.

'Maybe you got more money so you don't need to work?' said the hider of wetbacks.

'Nope,' said Slim.

He persisted in his dissection: 'How you going to live

without any money? You steal and you get caught. They'll throw you in jail. What's an old viejo like you going to do?'

'I got plenty to do,' said Slim. 'And ain't none of it your damn business.' Damn fool, he thought. Not the Mexican, but he, himself. For getting himself into this when he knew better. For jumping at the chance to get back across the border like a drowning man grabbed at the first rope. For letting fear and panic get the best of him. For seeing what he saw in the Nogales Yard last night, the big, smiling, empty-eyed kid in the train conductor's outfit, the same one who had followed him for two days all the way down from that siding on Massacre Creek. The one he had kicked in the side of the head to keep from getting grabbed. For leaving a trail a mile wide because he was in a hurry to collect his social security from the post office in Magdalena, three checks due. For not jumping off that freight right then and there before it pulled out. For changing his mind early the next morning and jumping off ten miles outside of Magdalena at the crossroads where a bunch of braceros were waiting as usual to get picked up by Fernando's truck and be smuggled north for the privilege of keeping salad on the table of someone who didn't know how it came out of the dirt and could have cared less. For being in the position that he was now.

'Hey — ' said Fernando. There was a nasty edge in his voice. It dawned on Slim that maybe he had jumped from the frying pan into the fire. 'Hey, I think I don't like you anymore. I think I'm going to have a look for that money,' said Fernando. He stood up on the dirt floor of the shack and gave a whistle and the room was suddenly full of his friends, and Fernando was pointing at him and saying, 'That's the pendejo who says he got nothing.'

They put the rush on Slim. They tore off all of his clothes except his underwear, ripped them apart, found nothing, grabbed him again and hustled him outside. He stood in the cold air shivering away his drunkenness and then they decided to take his underwear, too. That made them all laugh and Fernando said, 'I think we going to kill you, now, you dirty old gringo bastardo.'

That was enough for Slim. He took off running. Behind him they all laughed and laughed. Then there was a lot of noise and shouting and lights from the other end of Tin Can City and the whole bunch of them piled aboard Fernando's truck and took off down the highway roaring past Slim where he stood naked as a jaybird shaking like a leaf, not because he was afraid but because he was cold.

He decided to go back and look for his clothes. Someone put a light on him and said, 'Will you look at that!' He stood there with his hands covering his crotch.

They took him away and put him in a van with a lot of other Mexicans and women and children. It was the Immigration Service. He sat on the wood bench inside the van, a rotten old army blanket covering his body, jouncing down the back road toward wherever the hell they were taking him listening to the babies shriek against their mothers' breasts.

Then they had him out and put him in the tank of the Tucson jail and the next thing he remembered was that someone was yelling in his ear saying, 'Are you Slim? Is that what you call yourself?' And he was hustled out and up-stairs where a couple of tough-looking cops told him to sit down and shut up even though he wasn't saying anything. It was about six o'clock in the morning and the light through the venetian blinds was sharp enough to hurt his eyes. He rubbed them and scratched himself and when he looked up it was right into the eyes of a big, red-headed yardbull from Ogden, Utah with his arm in a sling and his face all bloodied-up. His name was Mulloy and Slim had been avoiding him for the last twenty years like he avoided all of them when-ever possible.

'Well there he is,' said one of the cops. 'He's yours if you want him. Phew!'

'I want him,' said Mulloy.

'You got him,' said the cop.

Outside the window a twittering storm of blackbirds was descending from somewhere high in the Arizona sky. They spread out across the sun-burned grass in front of the Pima County Jail and started hunting for something to eat.

The naked old man looked at the bloodied broken man and the policeman sitting behind the desk said, 'Will you get him out of here, please, before I retch.'

Mulloy said that he was sorry and thanked the policeman kindly and led the old crud-bucket down the fire stairs and into the fresh air where a few people looked at them but it was early and there weren't too many of them. Slim asked him where he was taking him. 'The YMCA,' Mulloy told him and off they went like the Lone Ranger and Tonto, his scrawny white knees wobbling along past the pawn shops and the *joyerias* and the all-night ptomaine palaces and the early morning brown-paper-bag crew. They got to the YMCA and Slim didn't want to go in. Mulloy gave him a shove and then had to hold him up. The clerk put the cold eye of death on them and Mulloy said, 'This man wants a bath.'

'This isn't that kind of establishment,' the clerk replied.

Mulloy said: 'You want to tell that to the Police Department.'

Old Arkansas said, 'I ain't taking no bath.'

Mulloy said: 'You want to tell that to the Police Depart-

'Well, you'll have to register for a room. Twenty dollars,' said the clerk.

That was fine with Mulloy. He signed the register.

'In advance,' said the clerk.

'Send the bill down the street,' said Mulloy.

'I'm not allowed to do that,' said the clerk.

'This is an antique gold pocket watch,' Mulloy said and pulled it out and showed it to him. 'It's yours for fifty dollars.'

He took a good, long look at it while Mulloy thought of his father rolling over in his grave and saying: *you no-good bum, giving away your family fortune.* The clerk said, 'Minus the twenty makes it thirty dollars.'

Mulloy said yes, took the money and the room key and got old Arkansas into the elevator, up into the room and into the bathtub. He wallowed in the water like an ancient Galapagos turtle, a prehistoric survivor of the worst the world could do, a living example to us all.

'Get up,' said Mulloy.

'What for?' said Slim.

'You're dissolving the enamel.'

'That ain't so.'

He stood up knee-deep in the dirty water and Mulloy scrubbed at the scales on his back.

'Turn around,' said Mulloy.

'Don't do that,' said Slim.

'It will improve your sex life,' said Mulloy.

'Ain't none of your business,' said Slim. 'Or anyone else's.'

'I was only kidding.'

'I had my share of women long before your time,' he said. 'Some good ones and some bad ones. You never can know which is which.'

'What – a clever fellow like you?'

He didn't bother to answer. He got out of the tub and Mulloy dried him off with the provided steel-wool towels. His body shivered when he touched it. He wasn't used to the feel of human hands. Mulloy wondered how long it had been since anyone had loved him? Since he had slept in a bed? He was a great veteran of human affairs, the last great white wanderer of the betrayed past. There was an urge in Mulloy to reclaim him a terrible, horrible sentimental idea closely related to zoo keeping.

'You led me a goddamn merry chase,' said Mulloy. 'You're lucky you didn't end up with a knife in your belly. You hear that? Well, I'm telling you. You gave me a real run for my money and now here we are, just the two of us, and when I get back we'll do a little talking and see if it was worth it.'

Slim wanted to know where Mulloy was going.

'To buy you a Tuxedo,' Mulloy said. 'And I'm going to tell you another thing. You lost me my lousy job.'

Sixteen-fifty of the thirty dollars bought him a work shirt, some baggy pants and a cheap pair of tennis shoes. The pants fell down so Mulloy tied them up with a shoelace leaving Slim's left foot a little loose but he rolled the trousers low. When it was done he didn't look much better, but he looked a little better. His hair was about three feet long. Maybe they would think he was the ghost of Howard Hughes.

Mulloy told Slim he looked like a new man and started asking him questions about what he had seen, what he had done and how in the hell he'd gotten himself mixed up in it in the first place. Slim wandered around the room like some-one from another planet where the meaning of existence wasn't a pay-as-you-watch television set. He opened the drawer in the bureau and came up with the Gideon's Bible which he looked at in disgust. 'They took my books,' he said. 'They was coming after me so I just left them there. They didn't give me half a chance. Real mean ones, all right. They took my books and now I guess I'll have to start all over again right straight from the beginning. That's a lot of remembering to do.' He looked at Mulloy. 'Don't know if I've got the mind for it anymore.' His eyes squinched up and a tear trickled down the seams of his face and got lost in the white forest of his beard.

'I'm sorry you lost your books,' said Mulloy. 'Maybe we can buy you some new ones.'

'Can't buy it, I wrote it. Everything that happened from all the way back.'

'Oh,' said Mulloy. 'Well I'm sorry.'

'In hieroglyphs. That's pictures but it's writing, too.'

'Well maybe we can do something. Maybe we can find them. I'm looking for a boxcar.'

'Lots of them,' said Slim.

'Can you remember which one they were fooling around with?'

'Maybe — ' Slim said coyly.

'You want me to make your teeth rattle?' said Mulloy.

'Wouldn't help none,' Slim said. 'Got them from a fellow who didn't have need of them no more.'

'How about some breakfast,' said Mulloy.

'Sounds good to me,' said Slim.

Mulloy looked at his watch. It wasn't there. Only the chain. 'OK, we'll get you some chow and we can talk it over, you can try remembering on a full stomach.'

'Looks that there arm of yours is going to fall off,' said Slim grinning at the thought of it. It was a statement of fact. It hurt like hell and so did the rest of him, thought Mulloy. Sleep, said the body. But the mind said otherwise and kept the adrenalin pumping up from the deep sewers of anger where the rats that lived in him twittered and glittered in the darkness of an empty heart.

'Well, come on,' said Mulloy and took him downstairs and down the street to a greasy spoon. He had a plate of beans and bacon which he mixed up with half a bottle of ketchup. He was used to trail food.

'Now how about it?' Mulloy said when the old man was done. 'You going to help me find that boxcar? What do you say?'

He broke wind loudly and all of the big city winos on the stools turned around and had themselves a disapproving look.

He licked a bean off his lip and said, 'It was a Burlington. They was taking stuff off of the Santa Fe and putting it in there. Making a lot of noise about it, too.'

'You wouldn't know the numbers would you? On that Burlington?' It was as wild a thought as Mulloy had ever had. Playing the slot machine because it was there. How many fish in the sea? Ask the dolphins.

'Of course I know them numbers. Get me a pencil and I'll draw them down,' Slim said.

'What — '

'Get me a pencil and I'll draw them down,' Mulloy went over to the cash register and borrowed one and gave it to him. 'I ain't got no paper,' Slim said.

'Use a napkin,' said Mulloy.

'Ain't no good.'

Mulloy felt around in his pockets and found a felt-tip pen.

'Use this and draw it on the table,' he said.

Slim mumbled and grumbled and made marks here and there on the formica. Mulloy didn't know what he was doing and didn't think *Slim* knew what he was doing. It was all a lot of nonsense. He drew some boxcars and some stick figures and some squiggles. The squiggles interested him and he kept adding more until he had a big block of them.

'What's that?' said Mulloy.

'None of your business,' Slim replied and drew some more.

Finally he said, 'OK, I got it. A one and a five and a one and a seven and a seven and a seven and another seven.'

'You're putting me on. How did you remember all that?'

'None of your business,' Slim said. 'It's part of my story so I got to keep track of them all. Which ones I rode and the one I got throwed off of and the ones didn't go where they was supposed to like the one that took me down to Massacre Creek. It was supposed to be headed for Flagstaff.'

'And the Burlington?'

'Couldn't tell you that,' he said. He had told him a lot. Whether any of it was true was another story.

'Come on,' Mulloy told him. 'We're going down to the Yard. Don't look so unhappy, I'm not going to let you get in any more trouble.'

'I ain't been in any trouble except what was forced on me.'

'How many men were out there?'

'Two,' said Slim.

'Well, one of them isn't going to bother you anymore.'

'I can take care of myself.'

'That how you ended up in the hoosegow?'

'How'd you know I was there?'

'I didn't. Not till they dragged you in.'

'Well, what was you doing hanging around a police station?'

'None of your business,' said Mulloy.

'Didn't say it was.'

'Wipe off your beard. You got bacon grease all over it.'

'Go to hell,' Slim said. Mulloy let him alone. They headed

for the Yard. The streets of Tucson had the bright and shiny look of a real estate brochure. Come to Arizona and be happy. Escape the mad, mad world one last time.

Down in the Yard Transportation Office there was a white-collar with his feet up on the desk. He was reading the morning paper. 'Hate to bother you,' said Mulloy. 'I'm down from Ogden Security. Wonder if you could check out some freight movements for me? We lost some traffic. Might be heading this way.'

He said he would see what he could do and cranked up his telex machine. 'Here, go get yourself a coke,' Mulloy said to the old man, giving him his last quarter. There was no place to sit so Mulloy leaned against the counter. It was pretty funny, all right, he thought. How they had both ended up at the police station. Mulloy was there to confess his sins and the old man was there because the Immigration boys had planned one of their extravaganzas in the war on wet-backs.

The guy came back from the telex. 'It'll take a little while,' he said, and picked up his newspaper. He peered over the top at Mulloy. 'What'd you say your name was?' he asked between yawns.

'Grabowski,' Mulloy said. 'Stanley Grabowski.'

'That's Yugoslav, isn't it?'

'No, it's Irish.'

He went back to reading the sports and Mulloy reread the front page headlines which said HUNT ON FOR KILLER RAILROAD CONDUCTOR. It was too far away to read the small print but he had a good idea of who they were talking about, Mulloy.

Chapter Fourteen

This is a memorandum. Two copies only. White House and National Security Council. Mister President . . . Mister Secretary: The Ivy League voice was sucked down the Black Hole of the tape recorder; it would rematerialize in a higher Universe where the Wizards of Power dallied with fate and toyed with the helix-chain of events, twirling them like so many daisies on a string as disinterested as Caesar in the fact that it was their own destiny with which they sported. Howard Matthiessen knew. It was useful to pretend otherwise.

I would like to say, first, that none of us here in the field have had the time to prepare a detailed report. The Director's Office is taking care of that. Second, that the Agents involved in the Canadian problem have been reassigned to administrative duties pending further investigation. Third, it should be apparent to all concerned that these men believed their actions were in the highest interests of the United States Government pursuant to the recovery of a strategically significant quantity of weapons material. And, last, that, if as we believe an attempt is under way to divert the plutonium to a foreign location for eventual weapons fabrication purposes either by a legitimate government or by a coalition of individuals with extremist political motives, then the problem will involve choices far beyond the jurisdiction of the Federal Bureau of Investigation.

It is our hope, of course, that the situation doesn't escalate. It is with this thought in mind that I suggest that a high degree of flexibility be maintained in our responses to immediate action stituations. In line with this we have re-

quested that blanket authorization for unlimited electronic surveillance be granted either by the Attorney General under provisions of the National Security Statutes or by direct Executive Order. Such steps are well within established guidelines relating to domestic intelligence gathering operations although certain technical violations of due process may unfortunately be incurred. Further, an effective method of containment must be developed to prevent inadvertent public disclosure of information damaging to the best interests of the United States. At the very least, disclosure will create a climate of sensationalism and acrimonious debate with consequent manipulation of public opinion by the press, special interest groups and certain prominent individuals. Since outright censorship seems impossible and since a declaration of emergency, giving the Executive such additional powers for the duration of the investigation, is an, I recognize, undesirable alternative, some other means of control must be found should security be breached. If not, our recovery efforts could be seriously impaired. To date, I believe that adequate interim measures have been taken to confine any leakage to previously agreed-upon scenarios. However, the risk of . . .

It was twelve o'clock at the Post Office Annex Building in San Francisco, California. It was lunch time. One by one, the mail-sorting machines were being shut down and the men who ran them were drifting toward the time clock like bored schoolboys with visions of temporary freedom from a spectacularly dull classroom. All over the city and all over the nation men gathered around time clocks with a similar sense of eagerness.

They stood waiting for the magic moment. A voice barked through the PA system, 'Hey, whoever's on number thirty-two, it's jammed. I want it taken care of,' said the voice. Everyone looked at everyone else. 'That means you, Colletti,' said the voice in self-satisfied tones.

A wiry young man with a Roman nose and an elegantly

styled mustache detached himself from the lineup. He said, 'Shit!' in a loud voice. There was laughter and additional commentary: 'You got the whole world in your hands . . . he's got the whole wide world in his hands,' said one of the Blacks. 'Right on up your ass, brother,' said Colletti.

He moved off, down through the long deserted aisles, the stacks of mailbags, the machinery. Thirty-two was assigned to junk – Third-Class garbage. Between the time that he had left it and the time of his return it had somehow managed to shred up a considerable quantity of valueless paper, a function usually performed by the addressees. The foul-up had started when the sorter had been confronted with a quantity of crumpled, waste paper that one of the bag men had dumped into the first stage of the machine. Colletti stooped, twisted, pulled and swore. When the machine was cleared he started to clean up the debris. Something caught his eye. It was the word BOMB, heavily underlined with a magic marker. He uncrumpled the piece of paper and read. He found another and read that, too. He became oblivious to the fact that his lunch hour was vanishing without a trace. When the man who ran the next machine came back he had a pile of little pieces of paper in front of him, all that he could find.

'What are you doing?' asked the man.

'Nothing. Mind your own business,' said Colletti.

'Just asking.'

The comment was lost in the din of a thousand men returning to work. So did Colletti. On the 2:30 coffee break he called his brother. 'I got something interesting to show you,' he said. 'Some weird stuff.'

'Got to cover the game,' said his brother. 'What kind of porn is it?'

'It's something else,' said Colletti. 'I think somebody ought to see it. You know, someone like an editor or somebody.'

'Yeah well, I'm sorry kid, I got to cover the lousy Giants.'

'I could meet you down at the ballpark after I get off.'

'Well, yeah. Sure, we can have a beer and suffer together.'

'I'm telling you, somebody ought to check out this stuff.' said Colletti.

'I'll see what I can do,' said his brother, the sports reporter. 'Tell you what, I'll drop over on my way.'

'Yeah, OK. I think somebody ought to see this.'

. . . that the diversion was carried out by individuals with prior knowledge of Railroad and nuclear materials security procedures is obvious. Both civilian guards disappeared with the shipment and one remains a prime suspect in this investigation because of known previous associations with radical student groups and his participation in certain other activities specified in the Director's Report. Deep background checks are in process of . . .

The man in the aluminum hard hat waved his arm in circular motions at the crane operator high in his cab and he yelled: 'Bring it up!'

The cable that dropped out of sight into the depths of the bedrock started its upward journey. A large crowd of construction workers had gathered around the edge of the cassion shaft. Their eyes followed what came out of the hole and then rose high above them to swing gently in the desert noon at the end of its steel noose.

'Do you believe that?' said someone.

'No sir,' said someone else.

'Then what are you staring at it for?'

'Because it's up there.'

'Jesus Christ!'

'He ain't going to help that poor bastard up there,' said someone else.

What they saw was the fossil of a man immersed in a large block of concrete. There was no doubt that it was a man because one arm was fully emerged from the breccia of recently hardened cement.

'Must have been in one of those cement cars,' said the inspecting engineer who had found him. All eyes swung down the canyon toward the line of hopper cars that rolled forward, one-by-one over the open maw of the mixer. A plume of white portland cement dust rose high into the sky and the empty hopper cars rolled slowly away toward nowhere.

'Probably some wino. Guess we better get some police down here,' said the engineer. He took the last swig from a can of Coca Cola, crushed it with one hand and walked away toward the half-finished dam.

What had once been Marcus Whittaker swung slowly in the sky.

... for whatever reason, the denial of our request for additional personnel has already caused a degree of delay and confusion in the exchanges of information between cooperating Agencies. Howard Matthiessen paused. He wanted to be clear but not too clear. His career swung on that fulcrum. *Mister President ... Mister Secretary: a cancerous situation exists which should be removed before it grows to unmanageable proportions ...*

'Listen to what I'm saying, damn it. The report was made yesterday afternoon. I don't care what those sons of bitches told you. It's their hook. They were the shippers and the goddamned stuff never reached us. That's right ... that's what I'm saying. It's either the Railroads' or the shippers' responsibility.' The man on the telephone looked out of the streaked window of the trailer in which he sat at the great rips in the Wyoming earth that opened like zippers to the coal beds beneath. 'I'll tell you this,' he said. 'If we don't get our dynamite by tomorrow, things are going to come to a crashing halt around here and that's no lie. Forty thousand pounds. How the hell they lost it I don't know. Jesus Christ!'

*

The glare of the noon sun had washed the color out of the sky, the desert and the faces that stared not at the world but toward some other reality whose components were the same pain, hunger and despair of existence seen in the faces of martyred Saints, relentless and crazed by the search for truth and love in a disordered and meaningless void.

'Brothers and sisters,' said the Angel of Death, the shadow of their destiny, the prophet of the Lord God sent down from the Kingdom of Heaven to stand among them in the land of their fathers as Moses had done, as the Baptist had done, as Jesus, Son of God, had done to shout the names of the saved and sound the trumpet of doom, damnation and eternal fire which was the end of the world.

The Angel of Death looked down upon them, outcasts, orphans in the storm of fate – the tools of righteousness and vengeance. His tools. His vengeance. He looked down upon them through the eyes of the man, the flesh and the blood and the immortal soul within. And the Angel of Death spoke through the man and the man answered.

'The light will shine upon us,' said the Angel of Death.

'Amen,' cried the man.

'The mighty shall fall,' said the Angel of Death.

'Amen,' cried the man.

'Fire and destruction,' said the Angel of Death.

'Amen,' cried the man.

'The lustful and wicked to Hell,' said the Angel of Death.

'Amen,' cried the man.

'And it was given to me from the hand of the Lord that I should be the instrument of this,' said the Angel of Death.

'Amen,' cried the man.

They all cried Amen! Amen! Amen!

Flies buzzed angrily in the silence. They settled to feed on the broken body that lay in the dust at their feet.

'I was sent down to you to lead you out of the desert into the green pastures. And I was sent down to you to save you from false prophets and from the sins of your brothers. And I was sent down to you as the instrument of the Lord God Almighty. In his left hand he holds the trumpet, in his right hand he holds the sword. And the sword is fire and the trumpet is salvation and the world shall end and lie in waste and ashes. For the word of God is in me. I am the Angel of Death and it is His voice that is my own.'

The man looked down upon them. His hands pressed his head as if the weight of light, heat and world which surrounded it was an ocean too deep for the human spirit to bear, an abyss of ghosts.

'Gomorrah shall burn. I have my orders. Yes, sir. The mission will be accomplished,' he said.

'Amen,' they said, the tools of his ministry.

And he looked down at the sinner in the dust.

'Raise him up high, brothers and sisters,' he said.

The sound of hammers on wood boomed through the canyon and echoed against the cliffs. Joe Morse ascended.

. . . concerning the possible consequences of such a device it is the consensus of opinion among the weapons community that neither the time, resources, skills nor knowledge is available to anyone acting outside of our own defense establishment. Therefore, the likelihood of an 'incident that would involve the detonation of fissionable material is remote. While minor differences of opinion exist with respect to the feasibility problem . . .

Matthiessen's intercom buzzed.

'Yes — ' he said.

'They got a confession. Down in San Diego.'

'I expected that,' said Matthiessen. 'What else?'

'That's not what he confessed to. It was an ordinary grand larceny. Breaking into a warehouse up in Barstow. Got the information from his father-in-law. Thought it was hi-fi stuff. It turned out to be tuna fish or some kind of fish or something. His wife got him out. Hired a civil liberties type. She made a lot of noise but they held on to him long enough to be sure he wasn't in on our thing. Too bad.'

'Very good,' said Matthiessen. He hung up. The tape rolled again.

. . . to continue, he said. *While minor differences of opinion may exist with respect to the feasibility of such a weapon months of preparation would be necessary . . . Packaging and transporting such a device would require . . .*

The noon freight for Grand Junction was going to be late getting out of the Provo Yard. This displeased the scheduler and his displeasure was multiplied and bounced right back by the foreman of the yard gang who had long experience in the art of placing blame.

'When they come in late they go out late,' said the foreman to the scheduler. 'You can wave them pieces of paper around all you want but it ain't changing anything and that's a fact. If they hadn't taken half my crew up to Ogden on some wild-goose chase the front office wanted done you might have got out of here on time. I'm not saying you would then, neither. What I'm saying is, stop waving them waybills and get out of my way.'

When the freight eventually moved out for Colorado it was a half hour late. Two locomotives and 130 cars clattering out of the Yard, leaving it silent and oppressed in the August mid-day heat. A sweaty, surly group of men clustered on the tracks watching it leave. The foreman stood there, too. He took out his handkerchief and blew the grime out of his nose. 'Coming from nowhere and going to nowhere, just like us,' he said.

In the dispatch office there was the faint click of a teletype machine. In the sky there was nothing but the sun.

The trucker picked them up on Interstate 10 just outside of Tucson. It wasn't something he did very often but they looked pretty pathetic, the two of them, the old man and the big guy with his arm in a sling and with a sign printed on a big piece of cardboard that said: UTAH FAST! He pulled up and they ran and climbed in. He was coming up from El Paso and heading for the Yakima Valley in Washington to deliver 80,000 lbs of horse manure to a fruit farmer. It was a long run and he didn't feel like wrecking himself on amphetamines. Just someone to talk to was enough. He told them where he was going and they said they were headed for somewhere near Cedar City. The old one kept to himself but the big one kept up his end of the small talk. After they had gone on for a while he asked him how he had banged up his arm.

'Fell off a freight,' he said.

'You don't look like that kind,' said the trucker. 'If you don't mind me saying that.'

'Well, you never know,' he said.

'No, you never do,' said the trucker. 'Nothing much up there where you're going but desert. And Mormons.'

'That's about it,' said the big one.

'Used to be Indians,' said the old man. 'They killed them all. That's what they did, killed them all.'

'That's too bad,' said the trucker.

'Don't mind him. He can't help it,' said the big one.

'Well, this goddamned world is a pretty screwed up place,' said the trucker. He reached over and turned up the volume on his CB set. Somebody was yelling about some roadblocks up ahead with smokies all over the place. 'We're jammed up for pretty near a mile in all directions in case anybody wants to know,' said the voice.

'Thanks brother,' said the trucker to himself. He turned off the four-lane highway at the next exit ramp.

'Whatever they're looking for I ain't got it,' he said and drove north through the cactuslands. It was a little bit of luck that Mulloy hadn't counted on. But they certainly needed it.

'Someone from the Bureau of Alcohol and Firearms Control,' said the voice coming through the intercom.

'I can't be bothered,' snapped Matthiessen.

'Loss of some dynamite being sent to a strip mine up in Wyoming. It was being shipped by railroad.'

'That's not a matter for us to deal with,' said Matthiessen. 'Ordinary channels.'

'Right,' said the voice.

'What about the courier?' said Matthiessen.

'He's on his way.'

'Good. Schedule a briefing for 4:30 this afternoon. All divisions and all cooperating agencies to be included.' said Matthiessen. 'We're going to establish some new policies with regard to who does what and why, around here.'

'Yes, sir,' said the voice.

'Inform those people in San Diego that they did a good job and have my lunch sent up.'

'Yes, sir,' said the ever-willing-to-please voice.

They had chipped enough of Marcus Whittaker out of the concrete to get at his wallet. The work was done by a state policeman with a jack-hammer borrowed from the construction company. It was carried out inside a shed at the base of the dam. When the wallet was extracted there was a pause.

'Well, get on the phone and call San Diego,' said the policeman to his partner who was young and not very bright. 'Tell them we found one of their guards and ask them what they want done.' He turned back to the task at hand. There was an ambulance waiting outside and quite a ways to go before Whittaker would fit inside. It was an hour before his partner came back and told him: 'They said not to move him.'

'Who said?'

'I think it's the FBI. They're coming up here.'

'Ah, shit — ' said the policeman.

After a long and silent debate with herself that had lasted through three hours of soap operas and the midday news, Etta Potts decided to make the telephone call. It was the quickest if not the easiest way of getting rid of something which had marred the ritual progression of the day. There was nothing to do but pick up the telephone and get it over with as fast as possible.

'I want to speak to Mr Morse, the one with the bald head,' she said. 'Is that the Railroad Station I'm talking to.'

'Which Mr Morse? This is the Operations Office,' said the woman at the other end.

'Well, whatever it is, he's the one from the FBI.'

'Oh, well, they left three days ago.'

'Well, what about someone else who wanted to know about Mister Jarvis?'

'Well, I certainly could ask Mister Dietrich. He might know. Just you hold on.'

Etta Potts chewed a chicken leg and watched Sharon Tolliver, the ex-wife of Frank Mason who had gone to jail for embezzling his brother's inheritance. Sharon Tolliver was telling her best friend, Marsha Hunter, that Marsha's lover had been seen with another woman. Sharon's voice was filled with venomous satisfaction.

' — Did you hear me, Mrs Potts?' said the secretary. 'The man you might want to talk to is in Las Vegas, Nevada. Do you want his number, Mrs Potts?'

'Just hold on,' said Etta Potts. 'I'm watching TV.'

'Well, I don't really have the time — ' said the secretary. Sharon Toiliver said, 'I'm only telling you this, Marsha, dear, because I don't want to see you hurt by George's failures as a man.'

'The number is — ' said the secretary, and repeated it. 'The man you want to talk to is — '

Marsha Hunter said, 'I know you're only trying to help, darling.'

Etta Potts said, 'That's Long Distance.'

'I'm sorry, Mrs Potts, but we don't — '

'I didn't say you did. Goodbye,' said Etta Potts, and hung up.

Marsha Hunter said, 'I'll love him until the day I die.'

'Oh, shut up!' said Etta Potts, but Marsha paid no attention, so she dialed the number.

The man on the telephone was blocking the heavy traffic to the men's room at the far end of the greasy spoon with the 300 lb waitress and the one-eyed Jackalope above the long formica counter. The man on the telephone was talking earnestly to some woman he called Pearl. She was obviously causing him trouble because his replies were frustrated and repetitious.

He said, 'But, Pearl, I know you're sick and tired of it. I'm sick and tired of it, too.'

The door of the men's room opened and squeezed him against the wall. A fat man with a string tie emblazoned with a genuine Navajo thunderbird glowered. The toilet gurgled.

'But, Pearl, if I do it, it's because I have to do it,' said the man on the telephone.

A father led his kid down the aisle and they squeezed inside. The kid was saying, 'I could have peed outside in the desert. Why do I have to do it here in this stinky place.' The door closed.

'So, what do you want me to say, Pearl? What is it you want me to say?' said the man on the telephone.

It was a noisy little diner, the only one for a hundred miles and the customers all had cameras strung around their necks and the same 'I'm not home' expression that came from watching what television called life. The road was just another show and the diner another commercial for quick hamburgers and the map just a TV Guide.

'Well, it wasn't always that way, Pearl,' said the man on the telephone. His voice was both angry and sad. 'Maybe if you hadn't done what you did I wouldn't have done what I did. But that's the way it is, so let's not talk about it. You want to know why I called you up? I don't know why I called you up, either.'

The door of the john opened and the kid and his father came out. They weren't speaking to each other. The kid made a face at the man on the telephone.

'You're not the only friend I have in this world,' said the man on the telephone. 'OK, you are the only friend and that's not saying much for either of us, is it? And I don't give a damn who you spread your legs for, why you spread your legs for, or what else you do and if you want to blame it on me that's too bad. I just called to tell you I could use a little bit of help. How's that for a change?' The conversation continued until it was interrupted by another man who said, 'We've got to get moving, friend. What did you say your name was?'

'Mulloy,' said Mulloy, who was the man that held the telephone. 'It's Polish.'

'What's in a name,' said the trucker.

'Not much,' said Mulloy. He looked at the phone in his hand and put it back on the cradle. Pearl had already hung up.

Chapter Fifteen

Eddie Shigata had tried to cancel it but the word had come down. Washington wanted . . . Washington said . . . Washington believed that . . . And so here he was in the convention center of the Sahara hotel speaking to a bunch of fat old cops and their wives and their kids telling them how effective and efficient the nuclear power industry was at policing itself and what the role of law and order would be in the blessed future of the breeder reactor and the plutonium economy. He had his charts, his slides, his films and his familiar quotations from the men of science and the men of power and when he was through with the performance they applauded and he felt sick to his stomach. Tell them the truth and they wouldn't hear. It was the parody of virtue that they wanted, he thought. The constant reassurance that everything was really all right. There might be some crime in the streets but no one was going to succeed in picking the pocket of mighty Uncle Sam because old Uncle was ten times too wise for that kind of thing. And weren't there studies being made to set up a national nuclear police force and a national data bank where the names of all the crazies could be put in the bulging vault . . . and maybe a few that didn't belong, but who cared about that when it was terrorism you were talking about? It was the parody they wanted, not the reality: the police chiefs of America, good men and bad, and like the rest of the people, confused and uncertain about what could only be called the process of History, the disinterested flow of events that scared the hell out of anyone over forty years old. And they were all well beyond that arbitrary point in time with sad eyes, shrewd mouths and skin the color of filing cabinets.

They had come to Las Vegas to have fun and to rub elbows with each other. Eddie wondered how much they had dropped on the Mob's tables.

He folded his tent and tried to steal silently away. But he was arrested by the Chief of Odessa, Texas and held without bail by his wife who wanted to know if radioactivity was going to kill her grandchildren because she had heard something about the subject from a friend of hers who had seen it on the news. Eddie assured her that the world was safe for generations to come – if not forever – and she shoved a glass of pink champagne in his hand and said, 'I know we must seem like a lot of foolish people to you but there are a lot of us in this world. We just get to wondering sometimes.'

She raised the plastic wine glass and peered across the edge at Eddie from under the blue powder shadow and the mascara.

Another hand found his forearm and squeezed gently. It belonged to a sleek young woman with circles under the eyes and the New York look. She steered him away.

'Mary Alice Taylor, NBC News. We've been doing the police chiefs. I've got an idea that maybe you could brighten things up.'

'I doubt it,' said Eddie.

'Well, there's always a chance. Just some simple questions and answers. The camera crew is outside.'

'I really don't have the time,' said Eddie.

'A couple of minutes? Might be a good thing for the Congressmen voting on the Energy Package to hear.'

'What kind of questions you want to ask?' said Eddie.

'Very general. We'll sketch in the details if and when it gets put on the air. Come on, Mister, make my day,' she said, and her face made a smile that wasn't.

'I'll give it a try,' said Eddie, not knowing whether he really wanted to or not. Besides, it was a good excuse to flee the merriment that had taken over the convention floor.

All they had to do was walk over to the cameras.

'Take!' said the man behind the cameras.

She said: 'Can you confirm or deny the reports that have

reached our news operation that a search is under way by your Agency and the FBI for a shipment of missing uranium?'

She looked at Eddie, deadpan.

How was it that the moment of truth had come to him instead of someone else? Instead of someone who was ready?

'You would certainly be involved in such an investigation, wouldn't you?' she said. 'So all we are asking is, is such an investigation under way?'

'I'm sorry,' said Eddie.

'Do you mean, No comment?' she said.

'No comment,' he said. 'Now let me out of here.'

'Cut,' said the man behind the camera.

'You sure you don't want to talk about it,' said the woman. 'It looks like a big, big story.'

'To which one would go to any length to find the truth,' said Eddie. She smiled her smile.

'To which I say, you are absolutely right,' she said.

'Hooray for all of us, then,' he said and picked his way across the endless parking lot with its endless rows of abandoned, super-heated cars.

He had been taken and he knew it. It was a risk of the profession, which was politics. It seemed that more and more of his job was politics. Less and less had anything to do with the moral and proper use of science and technology to fashion that better world that he and everyone had believed possible in the long lost days of innocence when Utopia seemed possible at the flick of a switch. Instead, the immaculate conception of the virgin atom had produced a Siamese twin, a circus freak of government and industry as self-perpetuating as the Pentagon, an empire dedicated to its own glory, power and survival rather than the needs of human beings. *For the sake of humanity* was a good sales pitch but the reality was somewhat different. A long-term reactor construction program could keep a lot of people employed and a lot of Congressmen elected. It was a patched-together, Rube Goldburg, sort of machine that had run smoothly

along in the ruts of general public indifference for a number
of years. Then the energy shortage had put it on the main
highway. The main highway treacherously smooth; the
machine had gulped it up, announced its presence with great
declarations of victory. And, now, it was about to run over
the nail that could tear it apart. There wasn't much anyone
could do about it aboard the machine and there wasn't anything that anyone could do who wasn't.

Eddie drove the car through the dazzle and glare of high
noon away from the Strip thinking of Jimmy the Greek
taking odds on this one. Of the country becoming addicted
to the melodrama which would be so artfully manipulated by
the men of the media. Of reporters everywhere running like
coyotes across the prairie. And, maybe, he thought, it would
be for the best. Then the people would know. Whether they
liked it or not.

He stopped at a gas station next to a Chicken Delight and
used the phone booth to call Matthiessen's office.

'This is Shigata,' he said. 'You'd better put me through in
a hurry.'

'I won't be able to do that,' said the cool, smooth voice at
the other end. 'But we can relay any messages.'

'This is urgent,' said Shigata.

'Just following orders,' said the agent.

'OK, then tell him this. Tell him that the networks have
the story. Tell him that the word is out. Tell him that if he
wants to know how, to ask them. Tell him that all future
inquiries will be referred to your organization and that I dis-
claim any responsibility for dealing with the situation in the
future. Got that? And while you're at it, tell him that we
would like to know what the hell is going on!'

Eddie slammed down the phone and backed out of the
booth.

'If you don't want no gas you better move that car out of
here,' said the attendant.

'I'm moving it,' said Eddie. He got in and drove away.

There was no place to go but back to the office which reeked of fatigue, tension and the nameless frustrations of inaction which was the result of decisions made at higher levels. The day-to-day work went on but the attention of those involved was minimal: they moved through the days as if in a dream world . . . and made small talk, and joked and laughed, and paused to glance quickly at the clocks on the walls to see how much more time there was before . . . before what? They didn't know. They waited.

Eddie's desk was stacked up with the work that he hadn't done. He started to go through the motions of an executive with things to accomplish. His eyes wandered, searching for nothing. They found a red, white and blue All-American Frisbee. He got up, went over and picked it up. 'Hey, Rosen — ' he said. Rosen was huddled over his desk befuddled with paperwork. Rosen looked up. Eddie winked. He tossed him the frisbee. Rosen tossed it back. Eddie put a little extra English spin on the next one and Rosen giggled.

'Let's go out in the hall,' said Eddie.

They went out in the hallway and tossed it back and forth and then they went downstairs and outside and threw it back and forth on the lawn. Pretty soon there were more people coming outside, first the bosses and then the secretaries and finally even one of the security guards got into it. And finally a cute little blonde with a great pair of boobs threw it up on the roof and the game was over and everyone trickled back inside.

Eddie lay on his back along with Rosen and Rosen said between gasps, 'Hey, I almost forgot to tell you. There's this little old lady up in Ogden that's been calling you.'

'A little old lady in Ogden,' said Eddie. He giggled.

'That's right,' said Rosen. 'Etta Potts.'

'Etta Potts,' said Eddie, helpless with laughter.

'Etta Potts,' said Rosen. 'Keeps calling you.'

'Well, by God,' said Eddie. 'I'll call her back.'

'That's what I call being a responsible public servant,' said Rosen.

'Glad to hear you say that,' said Eddie.

They got up and went inside. He was going to call Etta Potts but Chet Davis was waiting for him when he and Rosen got off the elevator. He hadn't seen much of Chet Davis in the last few days which was another problem. Chet Davis was the big boss.

'Come on, I want to talk to you,' said Chet Davis.

They went to his office.

'Close the door and sit down,' said Chet Davis. 'I might as well get right to the point. What you've done is — '

'What do you mean, what *I've* done?'

'Shut up and listen. You'll get your chance. What you've done is cause a lot of grief to some people upstairs and I don't mean just a few people. I'm not saying you were right or wrong, I'm just telling you what is what.'

'I'm getting the picture,' said Eddie. 'Matthiessen, that son of a bitch.'

'That son of a bitch happens to be the man we have to work with,' said Chet Davis. 'And I'm going to tell you now that you are out.'

'Because he wants me out?'

'Because I want you out. It's no good, Eddie.'

'And that's the whole story?'

'Not really. Even if it wasn't Matthiessen and his god-damned memos flying all over the place I'd tell you to get lost.'

'Why?' said Eddie.

'Because you are a news quote, my friend. They'll be chasing you from here to hell from now on in and that is all we need.'

'Granted,' said Eddie. 'How did they find out?'

'Nobody knows. Some San Francisco newspaper got ahold of it and then the wire services – and you know the rest. Nobody is blaming you for what you did and maybe it won't get any further.'

'Who's going to stop it?' said Eddie. 'What are you going to do, declare a National Emergency?'

'That's none of your business,' said Chet Davis. 'I want you to get lost for a few days. Really lost. Go visit your grandmother or something. Weren't you and your wife supposed to be taking a trip to Europe? Go do that. Do anything you want. Just stay away.'

Eddie looked at his hands. They were grass stained.

'You know how it makes me feel?' said Chet Davis.

'I'm wondering,' said Eddie.

'We'll talk about it another time.'

'See you around,' said Eddie.

'Go out the back entrance,' said Chet.

He went out the back entrance and found himself a bar. It wasn't much of a bar but it was good enough to get drunk in. When he was drunk enough to feel good and sorry for himself he called his wife and had a fight with her. It didn't start out that way but that was the way it ended – with Janet saying, 'I'm not the problem, Eddie. You are. You've spent your whole life wanting to get rid of your yellow skin. You wanted blue eyes and blonde hair so you married it. You wanted to be somebody who people wouldn't call a lousy little Nip. So you got that, too. And now there isn't anything left, is there? Well, is there?'

'I don't know,' said Eddie.

'I don't know, either,' said Janet. 'I'm going down to Ojai. The kids are driving my mother crazy.'

'I'll call you.'

'Let me think it over,' she said and hung up but the words went on inside his head making him feel rotten and lousy and mean. It was nearly five o'clock and the people coming in for quickies sensed it and stayed away from him. The only person who came near him was a hustler. She leaned over and said, 'Maybe you don't want it but I think you need it.'

'Shhh,' said Eddie. 'I'm evaluating.'

'It's pretty good stuff,' she said. 'My place or yours?'

'How about a discount in the interest of racial harmony?' said Eddie.

She laughed. 'Only if you can prove it's any better than it usually is.'

How they got to her place he didn't know and then she was undressing him and they were making it and she felt so different from Janet – like the difference between night and day, and her legs had the fine, burnished look of youth, not the heaviness of childbirth and boredom. He wanted to satisfy her. Not to prove it but just to do it. When it was over she put her head against him.

'What do you do for a living?'

'I'm a Kamikaze pilot,' he said.

'You got your discount,' she said.

'Whoopee,' said Eddie.

'Is that a put down?' she said.

'Hell, no. There was something . . . something . . . '

' "Something," what?'

'I'm going to call Etta Potts. First I've got to call the office and get her number and then I'm going to call good, old Etta.'

'I hope she doesn't mind a few alcohol fumes,' she said.

'Oh, no,' said Eddie. 'Not old Etta.'

So he called her. His last official act . . . but now it was unofficial.

'Mrs Potts?' he said.

'Miss Potts to you,' she said. 'When Oscar died I got my own name back.'

'Sorry to hear that. My name is Eddie Shigata and I am happy to tell you that I am at the other end of this line waiting to hear what you have to say.'

'I'd rather talk to that Mister Morse,' she said. 'He knew what was going on.'

'What *was* going on?' said Eddie, imagining Joe Morse in bed with Etta Potts.

'Well, that Mister Morse was looking for George and so I thought he ought to know.'

'What ought he to know?' said Eddie, sleepily.

'Well it was in a box and I opened it. You never know what might be in there, these days.'

'You are so right,' Mrs Potts.

'You just shut up and listen.'

'Sorry, Mrs Potts.'

'It was one of them counting machines.'

'You mean a cal-cue-lator,' slurred Eddie.

'No that's not what I mean,' said Etta Potts. 'I mean a Geiger counter. I know all about them from when Oscar was going to get rich off uranium. Never found any. That's what it was and it came by the United Parcel. They said they were sorry it was a week late but they had a strike on in Ohio where it was sent from. Of course Mister Jarvis must know all about them because he was in the Army. Used to talk about it. Then he started talking about God. You couldn't get him off God for nothing – not once he started.'

'Hang up, Mrs Potts. I'll call you right back,' he said.

'Well, don't make it too long. I've got to watch *Little House on the Prairie*,' she said.

He hung up. 'I don't feel so hot,' he said. 'I'm going to be sick.'

She got him to the bathroom and held his head over the basin and then stuck it under the shower.

'I want you to help me do something,' he said.

'What's that?'

'I've got to get sober,' he said. 'Can you help me do that?' She said that she would.

Outside of her window the streets were bright and glowing. The city rose up from its own ashes to flare and spark in the darkness.

Chapter Sixteen

'This is it,' said the trucker. He pulled over and stopped just where the road split into two forks, one running north and one running east out into the desert. 'You ought to be able to get a ride over there or maybe a bus,' he said. 'Might have to wait awhile. Or if you want, I can take you on into Cedar City.'

'Thanks for the lift,' said Mulloy. 'We'll take our chances.' Old Arkansas was snoring. Mulloy gave him a poke in the ribs and Slim gave him one back. They climbed down and the big rig pulled out and disappeared leaving them behind.

It was quiet. It was very quiet. The smell of the chapparal was strong. The sky was purpling-down and Mulloy wondered just what in the hell they were going to do next? It was twenty-five miles into La Vern and the rush-hour traffic was running pretty light.

'Ain't nothing here,' said Arkansas. 'What are we doing where there ain't nothing?'

'We are communing with nature,' said Mulloy.

'Getting cold. If you hadn't took my clothes I wouldn't be,' he said.

'I wouldn't have taken them if you'd ever changed them. Did you ever change them once in your life?' said Mulloy.

'Nothing wrong with that,' he said.

'Not if you keep plenty of distance between yourself and the rest of the world,' said Mulloy.

'If I had my blanket, I wouldn't be cold,' he said.

'Ah, shut up, it's not cold,' Mulloy said, and he took off his wash and wear coat and threw it over the skinny old man's back. Slim didn't like that but Mulloy wasn't in the mood to listen. He started walking down the highway toward La Vern. If the old bastard wanted to go in the other direction, that was just fine with him.

He went about a half mile. When he looked back Slim was still standing there. Mulloy kept on walking. The evening star was up and he walked toward that. A worn-out old school bus came roaring down the road going in the opposite direction. It passed him and he ate the dust. He had a longing to be back in Ogden in his mobile house surrounded by the ugly, the familiar and the commonplace with the refrigerator full of beer and the television set for a friend. He didn't want to be any different from anybody else. He wanted to go unmarked and unnoticed through the world leading a joyful and happy life. He would try hard to forget the past and he would never let himself think the thoughts that twisted him into a formless glob of anger and resentment. He would use alcohol in a temperate and dignified fashion and stop throwing his paycheck away on the card table. All of those things he would do. But he knew that he probably wouldn't.

A rattletrap pickup truck came along from behind Mulloy and stopped. Arkansas was sitting in the back surrounded by a pack of mangy-looking dogs. The man behind the wheel leaned out and said his howdies and asked Mulloy if he wanted a lift into town. Mulloy got in beside him and away they went.

'They call me Skunk,' the driver said. He offered Mulloy a chew of his tobacco and he took it. 'They call me Skunk,' he repeated and they chewed awhile in silence. 'Work for the Game Control.' He rolled down the window and spat. 'Take my dogs all over.'

'What do you hunt?'

'Whatever has to get killed,' he said. 'I'm up in here to get bear. Ain't supposed to be any bears up in here. Won't be any when I'm done. What do you do?'

'Not much,' said Mulloy.

'Well, this is the place for that,' he said.

The town squatted under its water tower like a half-dead sunflower. You could see the railroad tracks from a long way off. They glistened red in the sunset.

'I got to go tell the Sheriff I'm here, said Skunk.

'You can just dump us up there by the railroad station,' said Mulloy, and he did. When old Arkansas climbed down, the dogs made a racket like they were losing one of their own.

The station was locked up. There was a notice tacked on the door. 'FOR SCHEDULES SEE FRED AT THE DINER,' it said.

Fred was frying potatoes on the grill. It was a horrible thing to be doing to a man down on his luck.

'You the freight agent around here?' Mulloy asked him. He said, 'Yup.'

'Well, I'm looking for a boxcar that might have come through here a couple of days ago. It was a Burlington and Northern.' He recited the number – Slim's number – the one that the Pharaohs of Egypt had chiseled on the walls of his skull.

'Well, now, let me see,' said Fred. He went down to the other end of the counter and pulled a sheaf of waybills out from under the cash register. 'Now let me see here.' Looks to me like it was that one that went up to Jim Dempster's mine. Yup, that's the one.'

'What was in it?' said Mulloy.

'Nothing,' he said. 'It was an empty.'

'Well, that's interesting,' said Mulloy.

'Old Jim could tell you more than I could.'

'About what?'

'About them men up there using the place.'

'That so?'

'Lot of funny things going on around here lately. Funny things for a place like this,' said Fred of Fred's Diner.

'Like what?' said Mulloy.

'Oh, I don't know. It's hard to tell what people are up to. There was a fellow in here the other day talking to Joe and it turned out he was from the FBI. Wanted to know about those folks living up there around Indian Peak. Wanted to know all about them.'

'What happened then?'

'I guess he went off looking for them. That's what Jim said. Won't do him any good, now.'

'How is that?'

'Well, because they all left.'

'How do you know that?'

'Well, they pulled out of here about an hour ago in their old rattletrap of a school bus, that's how. Stopped to get some gas across the street.'

'Any idea of what they were doing out there?' said Mulloy.

'Sure, everyone around here knows that,' said Fred. 'They were getting ready for the end of the world.' He went over and gave the potatoes a flick of salt and pepper. 'I guess they just got fed up that it kept on going and decided to go wait somewhere else. It's a free country, even for those kind.'

'So they went off on the bus?'

'Singing hymns.'

'Well there sure are all kinds,' said Mulloy. 'How would I get ahold of this Dempster?'

'McBride's place. They call it a home for the aged but all the old ones get out of here and head for California. Except Jim. He's got the mine to worry about.'

'Mining what?'

'Memories,' said Fred, the chief cook and bottlewasher. 'You mind telling your friend to put his shoes on. Sign says: no bare feet Health Department regulations.'

Arkansas had both tennis shoes off and he was picking the scabs between his toes. It was a perfectly respectable thing to be doing in his social circles. 'Get up off the floor,' said Mulloy. 'We're going.'

'What are you looking for in that boxcar?' asked the great chef.

'Nothing special. The railroad just wanted to know where it was.'

'You work for them?'

'From time-to-time,' said Mulloy.

'Well, if there was anything special it wouldn't have been on that rotten old Burlington, it would have been on that other one, a brand new Chesapeake and Ohio. It went up there day before yesterday, I think. They been quite a few going up. Think there was a tank car, too.'

'Know what was on it? That Burlington?'

'Goddamn! Burnt the potatoes,' said Fred, and he went to work with his scraper. 'Yeah, I can tell you what was on that one,' he said over his shoulder. 'It was dynamite. About forty tons of it. Said so on the waybill.' He turned around again. There were grease spatters all over his apron. 'I guess maybe they plan to do some blasting,' he said.

Mulloy got the old man outside on the street and they walked over to the gas station. It was just closing up. Mulloy asked the man if he remembered the school bus. He said that he did. Mulloy asked him if he knew where it was headed and he said: 'I wondered about that. Most of the folks around here wouldn't ask them for the time of day but I try to be friendly toward everyone. Seeing as how they were leaving for good – not that I'm any more sorry than the rest of this town to get rid of them, coming in here the way they did with those women of theirs standing around most Sundays handing out their leaflets and hollering about God. It was enough to keep people away, until the Sheriff locked a couple of them up. That was quite a ways back. Nobody's seen much of them since. But we all knew they were up there. Fooling around with one scheme or another. They had some good ideas, I guess, and some strange ones, too. Like the children. Never would have believed it what they did.'

'What was that?' said Mulloy.

'Got rid of them. I mean, sent them all off somewhere. That was a year ago. Even the little ones, I gather.'

'See it for yourself?'

'No one did. It was one of them that told the county what they'd done. County sent down a woman to get them in school where they belonged. But they sent them off, instead.'

'You were saying you might know where they were headed,' said Mulloy.

'Well, what they told me was that they were going to Kingdom Come. Never heard of it, myself,' he said. 'But I figure it must be up near Ephriam.'

'What makes you think so?'

'Because of the telephone.'

Mulloy just nodded wisely.

'Phone company called down here about it. Said it was costing them extra because they had to run a line into the place. Wanted to know if they still wanted it done. I guess they gave out my number. Lot of folks do around here. That's because I'm always in one place.' He pulled out a handkerchief and blew. 'Damned dust. Well, I'm going to close up now,' he said.

Mulloy asked him where the McBride Home was and he pointed up the street. They left him there under the pool of the single floodlight, a man in greasy bib-overalls sweeping up the trash. Someday he would lock up the place and go to California to die, himself. The whole country would go to California to die in an endless suburb of lonely rooms with all their memories forgotten – Mulloy could picture that.

'You just sit down there and wait,' he told Arkansas, who was looking a little down in the chops. What the hell he was going to do with him Mulloy didn't know. What did they owe each other but a kick in the ass? Should have dumped him in Tucson, he thought. He needs nothing and wants nothing except to be left alone but the world wouldn't tolerate that. Him included.

The McBride house was an old place with turrets and bay windows and moldering gingerbread under the eaves. Mulloy had lived in a lot of houses like that, tucked away in an upstairs room while his father snored away his life. He had liked those old houses well enough as a kid to dream of sailing one of them around the world with its porches awash in some eternally warm ocean and him at the helm with the sails bellying full.

An old man with a shock of white hair and red suspenders was sitting in a rocking chair behind the rusty screen on the front porch. Mulloy could see that the old man had been watching him but he was pretending that he was still playing solitaire. The cards were laid out on an old lacquer-work coffee table and he hadn't been doing badly. When Mulloy played solitaire, he cheated. The old man looked like he did, too.

'You Jim Dempster?'

'I'm Jim Dempster.'

'I work for the railroad.'

'I know you. Knew you in a flash.'

'Where from?'

'About forty years ago your pappy was down this way and he dragged you along. He was working for the Railroad, too.'

'I don't remember it.'

'The kids ganged up on you and gave you a pretty good lickin' and then they tied you up and tossed you in the reservoir. We had a reservoir then. Now we got the tower. I dragged you out and you were pretty near half dead. Your pappy went down looking for the boy who started it and got himself into a fist fight with Splint, that was the boy's father. Both of them was pretty beat up so they decided to call it off. They went down and got drunk together and ended up in the lockup for trying to assault some respectable woman. Next day your father decided it was your fault and was going to whale the tar out of you but the doctor wouldn't let him in the room. We ain't got a doctor around here anymore.'

'That's too bad.'

'You were a funny looking little kid. Seemed like no one wanted you.'

'Yeah, that's too bad.'

'Well, I guess there's nothing you can do about it now.'

'OK, lay off. Leave me alone. That's enough. Do you understand what I mean? That's enough,' said Mulloy.

'Didn't mean to get you feeling bad,' said Dempster.

'I didn't say you did. Let's just forget it.'

'Sure,' said Dempster. 'What can I do for you?'

'You can tell me what's going on up at that mine of yours,' said Mulloy.

'Nothing,' Dempster replied. 'I need the money to get it started again. I've been looking for that money for a long time.'

'What about those cars going up there?' said Mulloy.

'Some other people. Rented them some space, that's all.'

'Well, what about them?'

'Couldn't tell you a damn thing even if I wanted to, which I don't.'

'There might be some stolen property up there,' said Mulloy.

'Reward? — ' Dempster asked.

'Maybe,' said Mulloy.

'How much?' he asked.

'A couple hundred dollars,' said Mulloy.

'Now let me think . . . what was it I saw going up there,' Dempster said.

'How about what you saw coming out of there?' said Mulloy.

'Well, that's a whole other story.'

'There's a reward for that, too,' said Mulloy.

'Must be more to it than you're telling me,' said Dempster.

'Show and tell,' said Mulloy.

'Hmmm — ' he said and reached over and pulled a card off the top of the deck. It was the Jack of Hearts.

Mulloy reached down and pulled one out of the old man's fly. It was the Queen of Spades. 'You ought to keep yourself zipped up or people are likely to think you're a dirty old man,' he said.

'Don't mean nothing. Can't make me tell what I don't know. Heh, heh,' he said.

'I can't but I know some people who can,' said Mulloy. 'Of course you might not want to be bothered. You know how those fellows are . . . They drag you off and stick you in a cell and then they put a lie detector on you and I've heard they do a few other things that aren't exactly nice. You know what I mean, don't you, Jim? And I'm going to have to tell them that you just felt you had to be paid for all the time and energy you spent sending that agent of theirs on a wild goose chase when you knew all along something funny was going on with those boxcars coming and going. Do you know what they call that, Jim?'

'I ain't interested,' he muttered.

'They call that a Federal crime,' Mulloy said. 'Withholding information.'

He had a can of tobacco in his shirt pocket. He pulled it out and fiddled with a cigarette paper. The tobacco got all over his knees. He said, 'I sure could use the two-hundred.'

'I'll take care of it,' said Mulloy.

'Can't wait,' said the canny old bastard.

'We don't carry that kind of money around,' said Mulloy.

'Write me a check.'

'I'm not authorized to do that,' said Mulloy.

Dempster smiled. 'Called your bluff,' he said. 'I knew who you was all along.'

'Who?' said Mulloy.

'A loser. Just another loser. You don't work for no Railroad. If you did, you'd have shown me your ID. You better get out of here. McBride! — ' he yelled.

McBride appeared. McBride was about eight feet tall.

'OK,' said Mulloy. 'You had your chance.'

'Run him out of here,' said the old man. 'I'd say, throw him in the reservoir like you did last time — remember that — but there ain't no reservoir . . . haw, haw! Remember that?' McBride seemed not to remember.

'OK, no one wants any trouble,' said Mulloy. He went through the door backwards watching McBride. He was coming through the door frontwards. They went down the path in the same way. 'OK,' said Mulloy. 'Go on home.' But McBride kept coming. He came at a nice easy pace with his big hairy arms and his big hairy chest under his filthy-dirty t-shirt. There was a kind of sidewalk that someone had given up on years ago and when that ended Mulloy moved out into the middle of the street, still backing up. He was trying to think of what to do but you never can think when you are full of the kind of feelings that make you walk backwards. The only thing he could think of was that if he fell down McBride would fall on him and he was trying very hard to avoid that.

'Well, well,' said a pleasant sounding voice from behind him.

He almost turned around but decided to keep his eye on the monster.

The voice behind him said, 'Looks like you got young Tom riled up.'

'Looks like it,' said Mulloy.

'Well I wouldn't stop moving if I were you. He can be a vicious man,' said the voice.

'I have no intention of stopping,' said Mulloy.

'I think Tom wants you to go that way,' said the voice. Tom, indeed, wanted him to go that way. It was to my left, toward whatever was there . . . or wasn't.

'Watch the steps,' said the voice.

It wasn't easy climbing the steps backwards. 'I'll open the door,' said the voice. He did and Mulloy was inside. So was McBride. There was no place left to go except where he wanted.

'Watch your step, there's a grate,' said the voice.

Mulloy backed up some more and then he knew where he was – he was in jail and the man behind him was now in front.

'Sheriff George Tate at your service' said the man. 'Don't call me George, I don't like it. You can go home, now, Tom.' But young Tom still wanted at him. But the Sheriff was closer and quicker. He slammed the cell door shut and locked it up. 'Now you get home,' he said to young Tom and the Hulk faded away into the night.

There was a long silence between the two men during which the Sheriff sat down in his swivel chair in front of his old, roll-top desk, took a look at the dirty magazine he had been reading, and rubbed his tired eyes. He swung around and their eyes met. 'You're safer in here than out there,' he said. He got out his cigarettes and lit one up.

'What kind of town is this?' asked Mulloy.

'Bad one,' said the Sheriff.

'Well, who the hell runs it, you or that old man up there?'

'That's our business. What are you doing here? You look like you been through a meat grinder.'

'That's my business.'

The Sheriff shrugged and blew a smoke ring.

'I suppose I've been disturbing the peace,' said Mulloy.

'I suppose,' said the Sheriff.

'How about a phone call?'

'Ain't paid the bill this month.'

'Lawyer?'

'Nearest one's too far away to do you any good. Besides that, he's a drunk.'

'Somebody for the arm?'

'The only Doc we had run off with somebody else's woman. All the way to Hawaii, I heard. Wouldn't have minded, myself. She had a set of tits on her you wouldn't believe.' The Sheriff's eyes half-closed. He was looking deep into his soul. 'What do you do for it?' he said.

'For what?' said Mulloy.

'You look like the kind that would pick up on anything,' said the Sheriff.

'That's me,' said Mulloy.

'Well, I get a few myself,' he said. 'Hippie types. Skinny and scared. I prefer a real woman, myself.'

'I'll bet you do,' said Mulloy.

'The best thing for you,' said the Sheriff, 'is a good night's sleep. I'm going to go on down and buy myself a drink but I'll be back so don't start yelling, if I were you. Makes people around here kind of mad. You're not that kind, anyhow, are you?'

'Oh, no,' said Mulloy.

'You're just a man on his way down, aren't you? No telling how far you might go before you hit bottom,' said the Sheriff, turning off the lights and leaving.

The springs on the cot had chewed holes through the mattress and the mattress chewed holes in Mulloy's back. The blanket had a history that smelled of the remote past. The moon was up and the shadows moved with it, slow and easy like the night trains, passing gently through space and time on the long, long journey. There is a beginning and would be an end, thought Mulloy. Being at the bottom of the well was as good as being at the top. Either way, there wasn't much he could do about it. The tiredness was making it all seem a little silly. When they had thrown him in the reservoir it was a form of sacrifice and it brought everyone a lot of bad luck. *That doesn't mean anything,* a voice whispered to Mulloy, and it was Sleep.

Chapter Seventeen

'Mrs Potts — ?' said Eddie Shigata. The long distance telephone line hissed and crackled with a thousand ghosts.

'It's *Miss* Potts and I can't talk to you now because I've gone to bed. Call me in the morning,' said a sarcastic and bitter old woman's voice.

'Miss Potts, don't hang up. Please don't hang up. Just listen to me for a minute,' said Eddie. 'I'm sorry to have to bother you but —'

'Well, then, why are you bothering me? I told you what it was and there's nothing more to say.'

'Miss Potts, what you have to say might help a lot of people and it might save a lot of people's lives,' said Eddie.

'What do I care about a lot of people's lives? I got my own to live and that's bad enough.'

'I know . . . I know it isn't easy, Miss Potts. But you don't mean that. You wouldn't want a lot of innocent people to suffer because you didn't want to talk to me.'

'How do you know what I want?' said Etta Potts. 'You're just nothing but one of those Nips and look what they did, you can bet your bottom dollar I remember. Bombing and torturing and sneak attacking, that's what they did. That's what people are always doing in this world.'

'Miss Potts, that was a long time ago,' said Eddie.

'Not the way I count,' said Etta Potts. 'I'll bet your father was one of them, too.'

'Miss Potts, my father was a gardener. He was in a detention camp during the War. So was I,' said Eddie.

'Well, I don't want to talk about it. That's none of my

business. You woke me all up now. I don't sleep so well. I'm going to have to take one of my pills.'

'Miss Potts, can you tell me a few things before you do that?'

'Oh, for God's sakes, if it means you'll let me alone, get on with it,' said Etta Potts.

So Eddie began. The hours of this night would pass away to be measured not in time but in a confusion of voices, the tired, the sleepy and the dream-haunted pulled from other worlds into his by the sound of telephones ringing in the darkness.

Some people sold soap. The Reverend Garfield Peabody sold God. There were still a few people around who believed in Him. In furtherance of his spiritual commitment and in conjunction with certain other forms of acceptable advertising, the Reverend Peabody owned a radio station located in the town of Hebron's View, population: 86, which had a view of nothing except a vast stretch of desert criss-crossed with dirt bike trails that led in all directions but went nowhere. The Reverend Peabody's program was called: *Garfield's Get-Together* and with the help of 50,000 watts and a certain lack of competition it did just that. It covered four states, twenty Indian reservations and a thousand all-night gas stations. They all tuned in because there was nothing else to listen to between midnight and dawn. Tonight was no different.

'And now it's time for a message, friends, from the good, church-going folks who fix the best country-style chili between here and Albuquerque, which is where their franchise ends. All of our franchises have to end somewhere, except the one from Heaven, let's not forget that while we're listening to the lip-smacking good sounds of Ma Honeywell's Home Made Chili bubbling in the pot,' said Garfield, giving the station manager the high sign. The manager let the commercial roll and Garfield metered-out a half-slug of bourbon from the bottle beside the microphone.

It was a stifling hot night. The bottle was half-empty already and Garfield was in one of his down phases. In one of his Red-Baiting, Witch-Hunting, All-American, Love-It-Or-Leave-It, God-Loving, Goldwater-for-President Depressions. He was in no mood to spread the Gospel, which was like peanut butter, nourishing but high in saturation and repetition. What he wanted to talk about was how the Government had found out about his extra cars and a couple of bank accounts he kept open under his wife's name in Phoenix from his days as a used-car salesman. So when the commercial was over he said, 'Let's talk about the right of privacy. Anyone out there care to call in on that?'

A lot of people cared to and a lively hour passed during which a wide variety of human experiences were mixed with a wider variety of prejudices to the satisfaction of all.

Sooner or later it had to get back to God. It always did. A lady in Wyoming said that she had received spiritual messages from other universes and that her sister who was near to dead from cancer had recovered. Another lady said that cancer was God's answer to sinful thinking – although not in the case of the first lady's sister. Garfield said, 'God works in mysterious ways,' and the second lady said, 'I want to tell you about my experience with those people at the discount department store,' and Garfield said, 'You call on in tomorrow night and we'll hear about what happened then . . . And now, folks, it's time for a message from that fine and upstanding man who gives you the best for the least, The King of Native Born and Bred Arizona Fried Chicken.'

Garfield drank his last glass of whiskey, told the station manager to get him an Alka Seltzer, drank it down, and came in on cue with a few remarks about the Internal Revenue Service. 'Now, let's have some more calls. What is your name, sir?' he said.

'I am the Angel of Death,' said a strange and hollow-sounding voice. 'Fear God and give glory to Him for the hour of His judgment has come. Gomorrah will burn. Repent before the end of the world.' Garfield made a cut signal with his hand but the voice went on. The man at the controls was in the john taking a leak.

'Blessed are the dead,' said the voice. 'For they have reached the Kingdom of Heaven.' That was as far as he got before Garfield threw the switch himself.

'Well, folks,' he said. 'Everyone has a right to their opinions but those kind don't belong on the air. Next call.'

'I'm from Cheyenne, Wyoming, and I want to know if anyone out there knows how to cure a wild goat skin? Shot it on a permit up in Montana. Indians used to know but I guess they're not enough of them around anymore and the ones that are left are too busy yelling and screaming about their civil rights.'

'Well, now, that's an interesting subject,' said the Reverend. He sorely needed another shot but the booze was all gone. 'Sure is,' said the caller. 'Wait a minute, can't hear you. There's a freight train coming through.'

The freight was an extra out of Denver. Denver wanted to get rid of an overload somewhere to make room for high priority traffic so they had sent up eighty-five cars that were in no particular hurry to make room for the wheat that was coming in from North Dakota and heading for New Orleans. Most of the boxcars were full of phosphate to be dumped on the overused soil from which the bumper wheat harvest was coming. Two of them were loaded with snowmobiles for a distributorship in Washington and five more were full of army surplus bought at auction and headed for a chain store operation in California. The chain store was in no hurry; it said so on the waybills: UNEXPEDITED GOODS. There were some empties headed back to their own territory and there were three gondolas loaded with rusty chunks of old automobiles salvaged by the Department of Interior that had been misrouted all the way to Kansas City before they were turned around and pointed West again toward a scrap smelter somewhere up above Boise, Idaho. The remaining cars carried the fortunes and property of a Chicago commodities speculator. They were full of soybean oil and they were going in large circles waiting for the export market to improve. When it did they would end up in San Francisco or San Pedro and everyone would be happy except the railroads who got nothing on the deal but trouble and would have liked the whole idea of suing them and their equipment for warehouses at low rates to be declared out of date with the intent of the ICC regulations . . . which were out of intent with a lot of things as far as the Railroads were concerned.

The Cheyenne Yard was being pushed hard, too, so the freight waited on a siding under a brilliant moon, a long, black shadow cutting a scar across the silvery prairie grasses. The men in the cab climbed down, stretched, took their ease. The beauties of the night sky overwhelmed conversation and, anyway, there wasn't much to talk about. Years of railroading had peeled away the outer layers of words and the quick emotions leaving a sense of quietness and peace of mind peculiar to men who moved constantly. Like men who went to sea or into space they had succumbed to the belief that they were a part of a larger process of nature and that their machines were more than just machines. It was a necessary but sometimes dangerous delusion, a transference of faith from the abstract to the real. The rails and the schedules were their moral code and it was as good as any other. When the two-way radio in the engine cab crackled and the voice said, 'You can bring her on into the Yard now,' they were obedient to its command. Like all men involved in circumstances beyond either their control or understanding, they knew not what they did but what they had to do.

For David Wiseman it was the end of a long and interesting day full of love, beauty, truth and power. The exploration of emotion always was. People were so different in their methods of coping, he thought, trying to pin down what it was that he meant. But the idea blew away in a hot rush of pure body sensation, all-enveloping and totally delightful. It was the snow, the little silver spoonfuls of it. Everyone was in the hot tub and they were all sky-high. It was a sort of reward for the long day's journey through other people's minds. Marin County people liked to take long day's journeys through their minds and they had the money and position to afford it. And David Wiseman had the skills which they bought.

He let himself slide down into the hot water until only the tip of his nose was showing. He felt like a whale, one of the whales that everybody was always saving. A hand exercised certain intimacies with certain parts of his body. A voice from outer space above the water was saying, 'Doctor, darling . . . Someone wants to talk to you on the phone.'

'Not now,' said David.

'Says you know who he is.'

'Not now,' said David.

'Says he wants to save you.'

'What does that mean?' said David.

'How should I know what that means? Maybe he's got the whole world in his hands. Do you want to talk to him or not? I can't stand here all night. I want to get in the water.'

'Go get the phone and plug it in out here,' said David.

'What do you think I've got in my hand?' said the woman with no clothes on. Her name was Alice. She was a sculptor. His arm came out of the water. He took it.

'Doctor Wiseman speaking,' he said.

There was a long silence. 'Well, what do you want and who are you?' said David. He started to hand the phone back. All he needed was another nut case. The whole idea was to avoid the nut cases. Let someone else worry about them.

'This is George,' said the voice. 'Do you remember me?'

'Well, that's nice, George. I can't say that I do and I don't think I can help you,' said David. 'I'm a bit immersed at the moment.' Someone had tickled him in the crotch. A lot of giggling was going on. His head was not too clear.

'God is helping me and he wants to help you,' said George. 'That was why I called.'

'Well, that is really nice of you, George, but I think I'm doing all right without His help.'

'Not after tomorrow,' said George.

'Why not?' asked David.

'Because that is when the world ends,' said George.

'That's very interesting. Just how is that supposed to happen?' asked David.

'I'm going to blow it up,' said George.

"Why would you want to do that?' asked David. Someone was splashing water in his other ear. A glass of wine had toppled into the water coloring it pink against the outdoor floodlights.

'Because of the voices, the ones I told you about,' said George. 'You remember, don't you?'

'Oh, sure,' said David.

'You said not to listen to them but I listened. The more you listen the more you hear.'

'Oh, sure,' said David. 'George – what was your last name?'

'And then you said I was cured and they sent me home,' said George. 'I thought I had left the voices there but they came back. They never left me alone. Then I knew where they were coming from. And then I knew why.'

'George, I remember you but I can't remember your last name,' said David Wiseman. His voice had risen above the chatter and everyone in the water was suddenly quiet. 'I just want to know who I'm talking to,' said David.

'It was His voice speaking to me, telling me what had to be done. Now I'm telling you,' said George.

'What are you telling me?' said David Wiseman.

'To pray for your soul, brother, so you can be saved,' said George.

'Thanks for the advice, George. I was just wondering . . . How are you going to blow up the world?' asked David Wiseman.

'With the Bomb, tomorrow at noon. Tell everyone to start praying . . . especially in Gomorrah. They go first.'

'Gomorrah? Where would that be?' asked David Wiseman.

'You'll know when it happens,' said George. 'You'll know and so will all of them inside their temples of sin.'

The line went dead. David Wiseman handed the phone up out of his hot tub. He closed his eyes. All around him people played and splashed. It was almost like a scene out of a Cecil B. DeMille movie.

'What was that all about?' asked someone.

'Just someone full of delusions of grandeur,' said David Wiseman and he let his mind drift away again. But the mood was gone. He was coming down fast. He felt tired, anxious and irritable. He got out of the tub and wandered into the house. He wanted to be away from everything and to forget everything. He decided to go to bed. But a couple were using it for purposes other than sleep. He ended up on the couch in his living room. Someone was trying to play his recorder and doing a bad job of it.

The old house stood alone on the crest of the hill cowering before the onslaught of the wind. Beyond it the badlands swept away into the darkness. The moon was obscured by the rising plumes of dust and the wind was cold, full of a sense of the great northern latitudes where it had been born. Rusted farm machinery and junked cars littered the eroded yard and the barn had long ago fallen down. A line of utility poles marched down the side of the hill toward the dirt road which led to a town that had itself almost vanished. It was a region of desolation and tragedy and there was no one who cared anymore and few that even remembered. When the telephone in the house rang it was 3:30 in the morning, but the old man was awake. Each day was the same so there was nothing to sleep for. Each hour of his life had been numbered so there was nothing to fear in the depths of the night. And every thought had its place and purpose in the divine scheme of things so there was nothing to grieve for – certainly not the loneliness or the devastation or the love of another human being. The old man had never loved another human being in his life. When the telephone rang he was reading the Bible. The only reason there was a telephone was because the company had forgotten about it. It hadn't rung in months. He picked it up, blew the dust off and answered.

'Paw — ?' said the voice at the other end.

'Who's that?' said the old man. 'Who's that?'

'It's George.'

'Well, what do you want?'

'I want to talk to you.'

'I got nothing to say to you or anyone else so don't bother me. I'm reading the Book. If you'd done that more than the other things you done, you'd be better off in this world – and – the next. Instead of going around and getting yourself in trouble and throwed out of the military, you should have read the Book,' said the old man.

'I don't want to talk about that,' said George.

'I told you you were no son of mine. I told you that. My only good son was fool enough to go off with you. And what did you do with him? Where is he now? Where is Esau?'

'He was sent to heaven, Paw.'

'To heaven? He ain't in heaven. Don't tell me that.'

'I sent him there, Pa. He was on a boxcar moving away and I wanted to call him back, Paw, but he had to do what had to be done and I know he's in heaven because I've been hearing from him,' said George.

'That's a lot of lies,' said the old man. 'He'll be back. He'll come home. You just wait and see.'

'He says you have nothing in you but hate,' said George. 'I don't believe that. I never believed that. This is the last time you'll ever be hearing from me so all I want you to do is tell me that I'm not all bad. Can you tell me that, Pa?'

'You want me to tell you what you are?' shouted the old man. 'You are a curse on the face of the world. I knew it the day you was born. You started out in life by killing your mother and you've gone on killing ever since. Do you hear me!' The old man cocked his head against the receiver, listening. It was a long time before George answered. But it wasn't George anymore.

'God has doomed you to burn in hell forever to pay for your sins. I cast you down into the pit. For I am the Angel of Death, the sword of fire, the destroyer of worlds,' said the voice.

'That's a lot of lies and blasphemy!' shouted the old man. 'No wonder you was in that mental hospital place! You ought to be back there, now.'

'Please Pa . . . Please! You got to help me,' said the old voice, the one he knew.

'Help you, how? No one can help you. You're gone, boy. You should never of been born,' said the old man. He waited and listened. But there was no answer. The line was dead. The wind must have blown down the wires somewhere.

'For exceeding the intent of his orders and for dereliction of duty . . . reduced to the rank of private and reassigned to the 11th Field Artillery . . . see notes attached . . . ' the voice of the Pentagon was dulled, half-asleep. It was 3:00am in the morning in Washington, DC but in Las Vegas the night was still being born. 'Given a medical discharge on 22 April 1972.'

'What about those notes, Sergeant? Anything in them?' asked Eddie Shigata.

'None of them are attached. Wait a minute, there's a tag. It's in his medical records. We're not allowed to release that information,' said the sergeant. 'Not without a court order or an attending physician's request.'

'How would I go about doing that?'

'I don't know. Find his doctor, I guess,' said the sergeant. 'Unless you can get a judge to do something.'

'Wait a minute,' said Eddie. 'Where was he discharged?'

'San Francisco. Presidio detachment. That doesn't mean anything. Hold on, here it is. He was in the Naval Hospital on Goat Island. Yerba Buena to you.'

'Why in a naval hospital?' said Eddie.

'They take most of the nut cases,' said the sergeant. 'He was probably a nut case.'

'Does it say anything about what kind of training . . . skills . . . that kind of thing?' asked Eddie.

'Sure – he had it all,' said the sergeant. 'Special Forces types always do.'

'All of what?' asked Eddie.

'All kinds of special weapons. Demolition. Communications and electronics. Went to a lot of different schools. They even wanted to make him a Warrant Officer. Turned it down. Wanted to throw him out of the weapons school. Got a letter from a General – it's right here – saying "In my estimation, Sergeant Jarvis is perfectly qualified to continue the course in weapons technology, maintenance and supervision without undue administrative harassment. I know what the policy has been but in this instance . . . " There's more if you want to hear it,' said the sergeant.

'You wouldn't happen to know,' said Eddie, 'what kind of weapons those were?'

'Sure,' said the Sergeant. 'Had to be Nukes. That's what the Warrant Officer business was all about.'

'When the telephone rang the General was dreaming that he had just hit a soaring drive which carried over a line of trees and then cleared a wide sandtrap before dropping on the eighteenth green in front of a huge crowd. Then the telephone was ringing and the General was answering and the voice of the base officer of the day was saying, 'Sorry to wake you up, sir, but there is someone who says he has to talk to you. Says if you don't you'll be responsible for the consequences. Sorry to bother you, sir . . . '

The General's wife was wide awake. She was used to the calls in the night, the sudden departures, the sounds of convoys moving through the darkness, the emptiness that was left behind. She turned on the light. The General sat up. 'Put him on, whoever the hell he is,' he said.

Fifteen minutes later he was in his office talking to Washington, DC on a secure telephone line.

'Well, I don't like to get him up unless it's important,' said Mrs Walker. 'It's his heart. He works too hard as it is.'

'Mrs Walker, it is very important,' said Eddie Shigata. 'I have to talk to him.'

'Well, all right then. You hold on,' she said.

Eddie waited and listened to the ghosts on the long distance line. He swallowed some more coffee and chased it with an Alka Seltzer. His head was a balloon and his stomach was empty from throwing up. The house was empty, just as she had left it, with a forlorn scattering of toys, overflowing ashtrays and a sink full of dirty dishes and all of it spoke of the emotional mess, the delusion and despair that had seeped into their relationship leaching away all that was good, leaving nothing but acid. Those were his sad thoughts on a sad night in August and they were as inevitable and as uncontrollable as the larger spectrum of events which his telephone was beginning to unravel.

'Tom Walker here. What can I do for you?' said the voice from Indianapolis.

'I'm with ERDA out here in Nevada,' said Eddie. 'There was a man who bought a radiation detector from your company sometime in July. What I would like to know is if there was anything else involved in that purchase?'

'Couldn't tell you off-hand. Have to go into the office,' said Walker. 'What else do you think it might have been that he bought?'

'I don't know. His name was Jarvis. You sent it to Salt Lake City.'

'Oh, that one,' said Walker. 'It happens I remember that one. Talked to him, myself. He wanted it shipped out right away. Sent it by UPS.'

'Well, was there anything else?' said Eddie.

'Well, not from us that I can recall,' said Walker. 'We don't sell explosives – just laboratory equipment.'

'What kind of explosives was that?' asked Eddie.

'Seems to me he wanted some shaped charges. Told him to try a dynamite company. Said he'd do that.'

'Any particular company?'

'Well there's one out in Kansas City and I probably told him to try that one. We do some business with them from time to time,' said Walker. 'What's this all about?'

'Just doing some checking,' said Eddie.

'Well, I sure would,' said Walker.

'What do you mean?' said Eddie.

'Well, he sounded to me like he was a little bit on the cuckoo side, that one.'

'What do you mean?' said Eddie.

'Oh, I don't know . . . I shouldn't be saying it because I'm probably wrong but he started going on about how he needed the equipment to measure the power of God and that the day of destiny was just around the corner,' said Walker.

'You'd better give me the name of that explosives company.' He felt a coldness spreading through his bones.

The town of Cheyenne, Wyoming was asleep. The last drunken Indian had pulled out from the last open bar to go home to his shack on the reservation and the last drunken cowboy had bedded down with the last drunken whore and even the Reverend Peabody's voice had faded from the black stratosphere leaving nothing but the rumblings and bangings of freight cars and the sound of train whistles to mourn the passing of night and pleasure.

The Railroad Yard was in high gear. Denver was spilling more and more of its overload up to Cheyenne which was already full of South Dakota wheat waiting to go down to Denver and from there to St Louis and from there to New Orleans and from there to the underdeveloped bellies of the world. Down in the Yard, no one gave a damn about the bellies but they did give a damn about keeping the traffic moving. It was a process that demanded the highest skill, the greatest level of concentration and a certain magical touch –

one that could wave the computer's wand over a stack of waybills and transform them into distances, delivery dates and what was called customer relations. Customer relations depended upon who the customer was, and who the customer was depended on a long list of determinants which the Yard Superintendent was supposed to be aware of and usually was. Some of this information came by memo from the head office and some of it came directly from the Inter-state Commerce Commission but most of it came from long experience. It was this that dictated what to do with the floaters.

'Just get them out of here. I don't care where the hell they go,' said the Yard Superintendent. His voice was magnified and it boomed through the speakers all over the yard like the voice of God. As the guardian of the nation's commerce and custodian of the Railroad ethic, the Superintendent had nothing but the lowest opinion of the people who manipulated the laws of his universe for the sake of profit and who made life difficult for all concerned. The floaters .. he knew them all. Lasky in Omaha who bought coal from West Virginia and dumped it when the price was right and some little town needed coal for its factory. There was the guy in West Texas who ran cars full of fuel oil around and around the Rockies waiting for the big winter freeze to drain power plant reserves, and that idiot in Las Vegas with all that Soybean oil. And there were all the commodity dealers in Chicago shuffling their pork bellies back and forth until the price was right. The floaters were a plague of locust and the way to keep them from eating time and energy was to keep them moving. He watched with great satisfaction as a long string of them were shunted away from their rendezvous with the Hump and its automatic sorting equipment. And a few minutes later he watched them disappear out of his Yard attached to the tail end of a freight headed west.

When the telephone rang, Jake Silver was asleep in his usual place, downstairs on the old-fashioned horsehair sofa in the parlour. His wife was upstairs, as far away from his house-shaking snores as she could get. It was the only wedge that twenty years of marriage had driven between them. The bed was still available for other purposes and, in fact, was used frequently during the odd hours that Jake could steal away from the floor of the Exchange where he brokered futures on anything that looked good to his experienced eye.

He picked up the telephone on the second ring and was wide awake. A lot of calls came at strange times in his business so he was used to it.

'Yeah, this is Jake Silver here,' he said and listened to what was being said from the other end. He scribbled some figures on the back of an envelope, listened some more, and said, 'OK, you want it, it's yours. I don't know about tomorrow, though. I'll have to check my schedules. Hang on.'

He turned on the lamp, found his Railroad Guide and consulted it and then consulted a stack of papers on the desk. He went back to the telephone and said, 'OK, I think I can get it to you sometime tomorrow. Where is it now? I don't know where it is now. That's the Railroad's business, not mine. So you want me to call you at noon, I'll call you at noon and we can take care of the details then. What's that? You want to be sure I call you at noon? You can be sure. When Jake Silver says he'll call somebody, he'll call somebody. Goodnight . . . Goodbye . . . I'm tired and I'm going back to bed.' He hung up. For some reason he was wide awake.

A few minutes later he was climbing the stairs headed for his wife in the bedroom. 'Belle . . . ' he whispered. She rolled over and opened her arms to him.

Chapter Eighteen

The door of the jailhouse opened with a crash and a bang. Someone tripped on the threshold and fell down and said, 'Whoa, boy, don't fall off before you climb on.' It was the Sheriff, feeling his wild oats, drunk as a lord. There was a woman with him and she said, 'Take it easy, baby. Where's the light?'

'Oh, we don't want the light on,' said the Sheriff.

'Don't you want to see the merchandise?' said the woman.

'I know it's mighty fine stuff,' said the Sheriff.

'Take a good look at what you're paying for,' said the woman. The lights went on and it was Pearl. She took a look at Mulloy lying on the mattress and said, 'Who's that? Is that the one you were telling me about?'

'Oh, he don't count for nothing,' said the Sheriff. 'Just a drifter. Come on over here and turn them lights back off and let's have ourselves a drink.'

'Don't you like looking at what you're doing,' she said.

'Just turn out that light and come here before I start getting mad,' said the Sheriff. 'I want to treat you like a lady. What are you laughing at?'

'Nothing,' said Pearl.

The light went out and the Sheriff said, 'I need it bad. I've been needing it bad for a long time.' Pearl said, 'Well, you finally got it.' Mulloy didn't say anything – just lay there and listened to it. She had to help the Sheriff and Mulloy listened to that. And then the Sheriff wanted her to do things and she did them. And then it was all over and the Sheriff was asleep and snoring like a pig and she was up and moving around in the moonlight, making the floorboards creak, making little sounds in the darkness.

'You didn't have to do that for me,' said Mulloy.

'Oh,' she said.

'I feel pretty bad about this,' said Mulloy.

'No, you don't. That's only what you're telling yourself you think you ought to feel,' she said.

'You didn't have to do it,' said Mulloy. 'Why the hell did you come down here? I didn't ask you to. I didn't ask you to come down here and do that.'

'I think it's about time you just shut up,' she said.

'OK, you are right,' said Mulloy.

'Where's the goddamned keys?'

'I don't know. Look on his desk.'

She turned on the light. Mulloy said, 'What are you doing that for?' She said, 'Don't worry about him. He's all tuckered out.' She found the keys and unlocked the cell. They went outside and stood in the fresh air.

'What happened this time?' she said.

'I don't know. I mean I don't know what I'm doing here or why you're here or what the hell this is all about but it started about four days ago and it's been getting worse ever since. Do you know what I mean?' he said.

'I don't know,' she said.

'I went looking for a boxcar and they fired me,' said Mulloy. 'I lost my job because they didn't want me out there doing it. That's the one thing I was pretty good at. And I thought, well, I'll just keep on going. Old Mulloy will just find the bloody thing and shove it up their ass. So I kept on going and that's about it.'

'What are you going to do now?' She was just a shape in the wind-blown darkness, another form without substance, no longer the object of sweat, lust and desire.

'I don't know what I'm going to do,' said Mulloy. 'You go on home. Get out of here. It's a miserable, bad place. Whose car have you got? One of the girls? Well just get in it and get moving. Just go away now. Here's looking at you, baby, and all that crap.'

'Something's happening to you,' she said. 'You sound like you're looking for the fucking Holy Grail.'

'Maybe so,' said Mulloy.

'Well, it isn't out there. It isn't anywhere,' she said. 'All there is, is rusty beer cans.'

'I know,' said Mulloy.

'Come on up and see me sometime.'

She gave him a quick tap on the shoulder and walked across the street, got into the car and was gone. They had touched. Their wings had crumpled and they had crashed.

Something shambled out of the shadows. It was old Arkansas.

'What are you doing hanging around here? Go get lost,' said Mulloy. Arkansas just grunted. 'I don't need you anymore,' said Mulloy. 'Go on, get on a freight and get lost. Go back to Mexico. Nobody needs you anymore.'

Mulloy pushed open the door and went back inside. He got the Sheriff by his belt buckle and stood him up. He draped enough of him over his shoulder to support the rest and dumped him on the cot inside the cell. His pants were still unzipped and Mulloy zipped him up. Maybe he caught a few hairs in the process. Mulloy locked him in and grabbed every key in sight. He turned off the light and went back outside. The old man was sitting on the steps. The Sheriff's patrol car was right across the street and Mulloy went over and got in. The key was in the ignition and the gas tank was full. He pulled out, made a U-turn and stopped in front of the restaurant. It was closed for the night. He hit the door once and it popped off its rusty hinges. He took all the Railroad waybills from under the cash register and they left. The lights of the town faded away in the rearview mirror like the lights of a sinking ship. He opened the window of the car and the night air rushed in. Mulloy pitched all the keys out into the desert. He drove on for a while and then stopped. They sat there looking at the stars. The old man started coughing and sneezing. He was catching all the diseases of civilization.

'You know where there's a freight office around here?'

Mulloy asked him. How the hell would Slim know?

'Well, I don't know if I do know,' he said.

'What do you mean, you don't know if you do know? What's the matter with you? Can't you answer a simple question, you senile old son of a bitch!'

'I ain't no senile son of a bitch,' said Slim.

'I didn't mean that,' said Mulloy.

'I know you didn't mean that.'

'Well, OK, I didn't mean it,' said Mulloy.

'Shut up and let me think,' said Slim. He thought, or something went on in his head for a long time. 'It's back that way, over them hills. Used to be one over there when they had a factory that was making ammunition for the war.'

'Do you think it's still there?' asked Mulloy.

'Well, I have a feeling it's there because everybody is still blowing up everybody else these days, ain't they?'

Mulloy turned the car around and drove back down the road through the town. There was a pickup truck parked in front of the Sheriff's office. There was a man hammering on the door. By the time he turned around they were gone. It was the old bear baiter, himself, the one that had given them a lift.

'I guess he saw us,' said Mulloy.

'He seen us,' said old Arkansas.

'How far up to that freight office?'

'About fifty miles, I'd say.'

Mulloy put his foot on the floor. The old wreck started to whine and knock. He was feeling pretty tired, too. The telephone poles went whipping by.

'I'm not asking you to release any information other than the name of the doctor who treated him in San Francisco – if it was San Francisco,' said Eddie Shigata for the third or fourth time.

'Well, yes sir, I understand that, sir. But I don't know if I'm authorized to give you that without further authorization,' said the Army private on the other end of the line.

'Do you think you could call back in the morning? There's a Captain in charge of all this but he doesn't get here until 8:30.' The private was pleading.

'Look . . . I work for the Government, too,' said Eddie.

'Not for the Army,' said the private.

'Look — ' said Eddie. 'If you make me wait till 8:30 it won't be me calling you, it will be the FBI and then you'll have to explain to them and then to your captain and to the general and right on up why you decided not to give me that name.'

'Well — ' said the private.

'Nobody is going to know anything about it,' said Eddie. 'Get the picture?'

'OK,' said the private. He gave Eddie the name. Eddie thanked him and hung up. He was running out of cigarettes and maybe he was running out of time. His finger slipped and he had to dial area code information twice. Then there was no answer and he had to start all over again.

'Funniest thing I ever did see,' said Skunk.

'Go over there and get that key and get me out of here,' said the Sheriff of La Vern who was feeling none too good, who in fact had thrown up twice, already and who was sitting on the cot inside the cell holding his head between his legs.

'Ain't no keys,' said Skunk. 'Like I was saying, it was the funniest damn thing I ever did see.'

'Get me out of here,' said the Sheriff. 'I ain't got time to listen to you.'

'Well, just hold your water,' said Skunk. He went out the door and came back with his rifle. 'Now, get out of the way. That's good enough.' It took two shots to blow the lock apart. The Sheriff came out and sat down in his swivel chair. He put his head down again. 'Water,' he said. 'Get me a glass of water.'

Skunk filled up a dirty coffee cup from the wash basin in the bathroom. The Sheriff drank it down. Skunk said, 'Well,

I didn't get no bear.' He squinted down the bore of his rifle. 'One of my dogs took off and I had to go looking for it. Found the funniest damn thing you ever did see. Found the dog, too. That's what I was after.'

'What?' mumbled the Sheriff. He was too weak to resist.

'Fellow up there hanging on a cross. Looked like they'd nailed him up. Can't tell you for sure. It was too dark, it was. That's what I came back down for, to tell you.'

'You're hallucinating,' said the Sheriff.

'What's that word mean?' said Skunk.

'It means you're crazy,' said the Sheriff. 'Nobody would do a thing like that.'

'Well, somebody done it.'

'Whereabouts?'

'What they call Indian Peak. Up there where them Holy Rollers lived. Looks like they went off in a hurry somewhere. Didn't even bother to pack up or close their doors. The ones that ain't dead, anyway.'

'What do you mean, dead?' asked the Sheriff.

'Well, there's about nine or ten gravestones they set up so I guess that many of them died. Kind of recent, it looked like,' said Skunk.

'Kind of recent,' echoed the Sheriff.

'That's what I said.'

'Go over and get my car started,' said the Sheriff, reaching for his telephone.

'It left town,' said Skunk. 'Saw it myself. Going down that street lickity-split, headed for the east.'

The Sheriff grunted. He jiggled the receiver. The operator came on the line. 'Get me the State Police,' he said. 'No, there ain't been an accident. Now you just do like I tell you, Louise. You'll find out all about it tomorrow morning.'

'I know, sir,' said the Sausalito Answering Service operator. 'But we are still not allowed to give the Doctor's private number without prior authorization. I'm sure you can understand the reasons, sir.'

'But this is an emergency,' said Eddie Shigata.

'I suggest that you call your local hospital,' said the Answering Service. 'They should be fully equipped to cope with — '

Eddie broke in: 'Just give me the name of his hospital. Maybe I can talk to somebody there.'

'Certainly, sir,' said the operator and she supplied the name. It took another half-hour of pleading, cajoling and, finally threatening, to get the home number of Doctor David R. Wiseman. The telephone rang for a long time before a befuddled-sounding female voice answered. 'Crashed-out . . . crashed-out,' she kept saying.

'I've got to speak to Doctor Wiseman,' said Eddie.

'You another nut? Some crazy nut called here last night,' she said.

'No, I'm not another nut. Just get the Doctor on the phone.'

'Don't get hostile, man,' she said. 'We're not into hostility.'

'That's good, I'm glad to hear that. Just find your friend, please, it's important that I talk to him,' said Eddie.

'What if he doesn't want to talk to you?'

'Then he can talk to the FBI.'

'That's a heavy trip,' she said.

'That's a heavy trip,' said Eddie.

He waited. Outside of the living room window of his house the eastern sky was turning a fruity, dayglow orange. It would be hot, and clear. The winds would begin to blow in from the north, the dry, hard winds that made people feel nervous and somehow vulnerable, like goldfish trapped in an undersize bowl. People would lose a lot of money at the gambling tables on a day like this. It was dawn in Las Vegas.

. . . and the sky was silver-gray over the siding at Spanish Fork where lines of boxcars stood glistening with early morning dew. They had come in from Rock Springs during the night. Some of them would stand for days. Others would go north to Salt Lake City. Some would move south. The men who worked the siding were drinking coffee inside a derailed caboose. There was a teletype machine and a telephone and a portable radio. The radio was warning the world of the imminent perils of acid indigestion and offering speedy relief. Then it played the bottom of the top-ten and then the announcer's voice said, 'This is a test of your Civil Defense Emergency Network. In case of a real emergency stay tuned to this station. Thirty seconds of silence will follow. I repeat, this is a test.'

'They ought to test the water around here,' said one of the men who were drinking coffee. He grimaced but swallowed what was left in his cup. The teletype machine began to chatter. When it stopped he got up and read what was there.

'I guess we have to go to work, boys. They want them tank cars moved out,' he said.

Chapter Nineteen

For Howard Matthiessen the night had been a torment. It had wrecked his career, betrayed him, left him without confidence. Now he stood shivering in the dawn surrounded by subordinates, advisors and military equipment looking up the dirt road that led into the gray and dessicated mountains. Somewhere up there was a place called Hope, and in that place was the man who was responsible for his catastrophe. The man who had been clever enough and lucky enough to succeed where others would most certainly have failed. The man who twisted the threads of the investigation into knots and who had fooled the internal security system of an entire nation for several days and who might have fooled it even longer if his objectives had been rational, his motives, sane. The man with the plutonium . . . the man and the people up there with him, all of them nothing more than social wreckage, the kind who crawled out of holes after dark to get even with the world for their low position in it. That was what Howard Matthiessen thought. It was angry, bitter, judgmental reasoning. Like the man up there, he had become a victim of his own self-deceit.

A soldier in combat fatigues approached. He was a colonel. 'We're ready,' was all that he said, all that needed to be said. With a nod from Matthiessen the convoy moved off up the road. The dust rose behind the armored personnel carriers, the jeeps and the canvas-covered trucks. The cars with the agents followed. The highway that they had left was deserted. The State Police had thrown up road blocks for forty miles in either direction. The convoy wound up into the

mountains and vanished leaving nothing but the silence and
the desert and the smoldering embers of a badly stamped-out
cigarette and an odor that was hard to identify unless you
knew war. It was the smell of fear.

The soldiers had been reassured. Matthiessen had been
reassured. Everyone had been reassured by the man who
had arrived from Los Alamos and who was with them now,
the young-but-running-to-middle-aged man with the glasses
and the nasal, high-pitched voice.

'We have a firm consensus from everyone at the establishment on this,' he had said. 'There is absolutely no possibility
that a weapon could have been fabricated given the time
allowed and, of course, given the people involved. I'll tell
you something, gentlemen. If I had the stuff, it would take
months . . . Months to fabricate any kind of nuclear device
with a reasonable yield efficiency. Meaning that I would
start from scratch.'

'What if they didn't start from scratch?' Chet Davis had
asked.

'You read a lot of baloney about that and you know it's
baloney too,' said the man from Los Alamos. 'It takes time,
it takes a lot of education and it takes a lot of components.
You give me a hundred high school physics students and I'll
give you a hundred fizzles. One hundred – and I'm willing to
stake money on that.'

'How big would the fizzles be?' asked Chet Davis. 'Five
kilotons . . . Ten kilotons?'

'That's a loaded question and you know it,' said the man
from Los Alamos. 'It's a distortion of the facts applicable to
this situation.'

And the meeting had broken up. Now they were all riding
in the car up the mountain toward the place where the telephone call had emanated, the call which the Commanding
General of Fort Bragg, North Carolina had reported
immediately to the Federal Bureau of Investigation as a hoax
but, nevertheless, a threat to National Security worthy of
their attention since it involved a hysterical bomb threat by
an individual who called himself the Angel of Death and

who had told the General that the fury of God was about to be unleashed, that no power on earth could stop it. An hour later, Matthiessen was talking to him and the General said, as he had said before, 'Don't know if there is anything to it but he gave me a telephone number. Said he was hoping I'd get in touch with the President and that if the President wanted to call him he'd lead him in prayer before the end. I don't know what he meant by that. Maybe he's a suicidal maniac. Plenty of them around these days. At any rate, I've done my job. I'm sure you fellows will take care of it from here. There's only one thing that leaves me in the dark.'

'What's that?' Matthiessen had asked.

'Why the hell did he call me? We don't have any men like that in this man's army. Certainly not in the Special Forces,' the General had said in genuine bewilderment.

At least the cards were on the table. There was no more confusion, uncertainty or disagreement. There was only the tension of accomplishing the mission. When they departed the Federal Building in Las Vegas there were no reporters about. The San Francisco leak had been plugged. The offending notes from the mailbag that had found its way out into the world from Ogden had been collected by agents posing as Post Office investigators. The wire services and the networks had been told that it was part of a training scenario put together by the Pentagon and the Justice Department, a simple exercise in preparedness. This had been verified by a White House spokesman. The story was dead. The important thing was to keep it buried and to salvage what could be salvaged from the wreckage of the investigation. Filled with such sanguine thoughts Matthiessen rode up into the mountains. His instructions had been given. There was nothing more to say.

'Chet Davis,' said Eddie. 'Right away.'

'I'm sorry,' said the switchboard. 'He's not in the building. Did you try his home number?'

'He's not there,' said Eddie.

'You might try the Federal Offices,' said the switchboard. 'He was in a meeting late last night.'

'Thanks,' said Eddie. He hung up. He called the FBI for the second time. 'Listen,' he said. 'I've got to get hold of him. If he isn't there, I'll speak to anyone. Let me talk to Matthiessen.'

'I'm sorry, sir,' said the switchboard. 'Mister Matthiessen is unavailable at this time. You might try later.'

'Well, who's in charge? Didn't he leave someone in charge?'

'There are no agents in the building at the present time, said the switchboard.

'I've got to talk to someone,' said Eddie.

'Hold on, please,' said the switchboard in a very irritable tone of voice. A minute passed. Eddie was about to hang up when a connection was made. It was a tired-sounding guy with the Bureau of Firearms and Alcohol Control, someone named Sullivan. He was going to be of no help at all. Eddie was about to hang up again when something occurred to him: 'I don't know if you would know anything about this, but I'm in the process of tracing some high-explosives that were shipped out of Kansas City.'

'That's interesting,' said Sullivan. 'So am I. And I think I've found them.'

'Fifty shaped charges made up to order for someone named Jarvis?'

'Nope,' said Sullivan. 'I'm looking for 40,000 lbs of dynamite that got lost on the railroad.'

'Where was it going?' said Eddie.

'Up to a strip mine that run out of what they usually use, an on-site mix,' said Sullivan. 'Been missing for three days. Got lost going out of Ogden.'

'You said you think you've found it?' said Eddie.

'I said I think I know where it is.'

'I think you'd better tell me,' said Eddie.

'I don't see that it's any of your business.'

'The shaped charges went to a post office box at a place called La Vern, Utah.'

'Maybe we ought to have a little chat,' said Sullivan.

'There isn't any time for that. Is that where that dynamite ended up? Is that where it is?'

'Well, that's what they told me. Said they'd figured it out. Somebody had made a mistake feeding in information to the computer. I'm going up there myself this morning,' said Sullivan.

'I don't think you'll find it,' said Eddie.

'That's where it is,' said Sullivan.

'That is where it was sent – deliberately,' said Eddie.

'I had a feeling . . . ' said Sullivan. 'Tried to talk to that bunch of agents who have been hanging around here but they said they didn't have the time. Well, I suppose there's nothing I can do but go up there anyway. It's not too far. Maybe a hundred miles.'

'You wouldn't have any idea where that group of agents went?'

'Out to Nellis Air Force Base. Never saw so many people moving so quick.'

'Thanks,' said Eddie.

'I didn't mean it to be such bad news,' said Sullivan. 'Anything I can do?'

'No,' said Eddie. 'I don't think there's much that anybody can do.'

'Well, don't worry about the dynamite.'

'What do you mean?' said Eddie.

'It won't go off accidentally,' said Sullivan.

Now the colors of the dawn had faded to be replaced by the harsh reflection of light on rock. The wind had come to dance in the misshapen pines that crowned the high ridges and the sky hung over it all, a transparency without beginning or end. The corpse of Hope lay under this shroud of time and space. It had died fifty years ago. The desert had mummified it. Even the school bus parked in front of the church seemed permanent, like an offering left in front of a tomb. The silence was complete. Nothing moved. The convoy was in position.

'About two minutes,' someone whispered to Matthiessen. It was the Colonel again. He was chewing a wad of tobacco. He had keen, gray, level eyes. There was nothing in the world, they said, that he was afraid of.

'Proceed when ready,' said Matthiessen. The sweat from the hike up the road was evaporating. He felt chilled. The church was down below at the far end of what had once been a street. A part of the roof had blown off but the steeple still stood, tall and straight. All of the stained glass was gone. The windows were empty. The telephone line came in off a new utility pole. A bird sat on top of the pole preening itself. When the singing started it flew away.

The hymn started softly, a scattering of voices that searched and found each other and found strength as well until the sound rolled out through the gaping windows of the church filling the world with pride in the power of faith and the strength of God. It was 'Rock of Ages'. The voices faded away and all was silent.

Then the amplified voice of a soldier boomed. 'This is the United States Government. You are surrounded. You have one minute to surrender yourselves. Come out with your hands up. You will not be harmed. You have one minute . . .'

A hundred eyes looked at a hundred watches and waited. Behind the town the sun had just risen over the mountain. The glare filled the valley, charging it with a great force that stretched the moments into some other category of time where a million years was nothing.

A soldier scurried forward and another and another. The spell was broken. The street below was suddenly alive with moving men. The church stood silent, steeple pointing at the sky. Then, in a concussive flash that was brighter than the sunlight it disappeared – vanished instantly from the face of the earth. The sky was shattered and from it a dark rain of debris fell on shouting, screaming men. High in the sky the cupola of a steeple rotated slowly and then fell back to earth to break in a thousand pieces. Then, except for the whimpering of a wounded man, all was silent again. The Angel of Death had spoken.

Amidst a shambles of dust, confusion and the gunpowder stench of high explosive the men with the radiation counters hurried forward. Chester Davis sat on a rock and prayed. Howard Matthiessen just stood. The Army colonel rose from the spot where he had flung himself on the ground and began meticulously to brush himself off. It was too late to run. It was too late to do anything except to wait to see if they were all dead men, to see if the gray cloud that rose high into the sky where the winds were already scattering it in long streamers far to the south was full of plutonium particles, the bacteria of atomic degeneration, the bearers of a plague more horrible than nature would ever have dared invent.

The word was not long in coming. 'A normal background count,' said a soldier who had run up the hill to salute the Colonel and bring the news. 'It was just dynamite, sir. They blew themselves up with dynamite.'

The soldier waited for a reaction. There was none. The colonel was trying to light his pipe but the matches kept going out. Finally, he stuck it in his mouth and clamped down hard. The sound of men and machines filled the air. Where the church had stood there was a crater – nothing more. Where the school bus had stood there was a smolder-ing pile of metal. Some of the other buildings in the ghost town had caught fire. There was no way to put them out so they burned adding a column of black smoke to the already gray sky.

Another soldier came panting up from the rear. He found Chester Davis and handed him a message. Davis read it, got up off his rock and walked over to Matthiessen and gave it to him. Matthiessen took it, held it up and squinted at the words. When he was through his hand dropped and the piece of paper fluttered away.

The message said: HAD THE KNOW HOW. HAS THE BOMB. ACCORDING AUTHORITATIVE SOURCE, MOST LIKELY TARGET SALT LAKE CITY NOON TODAY. TOO BIG TO MOVE EXCEPT BY RAIL. DO NOT JEOPARDIZE

CHANCE OF RECOVERY. CONFIRM. SHIGATA.

An injured man was being led toward a helicopter. The time was 8:00am.

At the Chicago Board of Trade it was 10:00am and the futures market had just begun. Jake Silver moved slowly across the floor toward one of the pits where his colleagues clustered around a man who was chalking opening prices on a small blackboard. The mood was casual, the level of interest as low as the cloudy skies over Lake Michigan. The market was in retreat. There were too many troubles in the world. A lot of options would go unbid until something happened to stimulate optimism if not confidence in the future buying power of America and the future policies of several foreign countries where such things as gold was mined and perhaps coffee grown.

Jake elbowed his way into the group, traded gossip with a number of men, told a joke or two, was invited to a wedding and asked by an earnest young hustler if he wanted to get rid of his soybean oil?

'It's sold,' said Jake.

'How much?' said the kid.

'Get lost,' said Jake.

'I'll give you another couple of points,' said the hustler. 'I got a customer.'

'You got a customer, I got a customer. Get lost,' said Jake, but with less conviction. A rapid mental calculation had gone on in his head. The kid was talking about an extra $12,000 on the shipment.

'Come on, come on,' said the kid. 'You want the action?'

'I can't tell you till noon,' said Jake.

'What do you mean, noon? I can't wait till noon,' said the hustler.

'That's the best I can do,' said Jake. He was an honest man. A deal was a deal. Unless he could wriggle out from under it. 'Wait a minute,' he told the hustler. 'I'll go call the guy now.' Jake left the pit. He walked over to the other side of the floor to the bank of telephones rented by the Exchange for the use of its members. Maybe the guy had changed his mind. It was always worth a try. He dialed the number.

The ringing had a pervasive, faraway sound like white noise. It was white noise, thought Eddie. White, white . . . Like smoke from a chimney in a Japanese landscape. His head was pressing against something. It was the desk. He had fallen asleep. He jerked himself up and answered the telephone.

'You wanted me to call you back after I checked our shipping records?' It was the United Parcel Service.

'Find out anything?' asked Eddie. He tried to focus on something, to concentrate.

'Well the only other thing was a couple of car telephones,' said the man from United Parcel. 'I guess he was one of them – what do you call it – them do-it-yourselfers. Bought them from some outfit called Ten-Four Communications down in Salt Lake City.'

'You mean radio telephones?' said Eddie.

'All I know is what it says.'

'Sure,' said Eddie.

When he called Ten-Four Communications the voice that answered was a machine. It said: 'This is a recording. No one is in the office at the moment. Be sure to leave your name and number and we will call you back . . . Wait for the tone . . .'

'This is an urgent message — ' Eddie said. He stopped, looked at the receiver and slammed it down. Nobody wanted to know. Nobody could be bothered. Nobody wanted to listen. Nobody was going to do anything. Nobody cared one way or another.

'You dumb sons of bitches, don't you understand? You're all going to get blown to hell and there is nothing I can do about it,' said Eddie Shigata.

Outside of his window there was a hissing sound. The

automatic lawn sprinkler system had turned itself on. When he had regained control of himself he dialed the number again and left his message.

'What do you mean, this number isn't in service?' said Jake Silver. There was an ashtray full of dead cigar butts. He picked one up, looked at it attentively, and put it back down. 'That's right, it's a 702 Area Code . . . ' He mimicked her voice. He took a fresh cigar out of his own shirt pocket and appraised it. He had promised Belle: one in the morning, two in the afternoon and one at night. 'Listen, little girlie, I wasn't making fun of you. My name is Jake Silver and I'm sixty-three years old and God bless us that we should all live to be ninety. Maybe you could just check out this number for me and make me a happy man. You could? Well that's a nice thing to do. What's your name, little girl? Helen – I've got a cousin named Helen. Maybe you wouldn't mind calling me back,' said Jake. 'I'm a very busy man.' They exchanged further information and more pleasantries and Jake put down the telephone. He stared at the cigar. The hell with it, he thought, and struck a match.

Three men were in the process of determining the possibilities of survival for several hundred thousand people. Two of them squatted on their heels and drew crude pictures in the sand with dead bits of mesquite. The third was standing up and he was Howard Matthiessen. His attention was fragmented – scattered like the pieces of the church on a wind of events that was blowing everything in the world toward the edge of a cliff.

The weapons scientist from Los Alamos was saying: 'I personally doubt that he has the technical qualifications to make that kind of assessment.'

Chet Davis said, 'What do you think it takes, a special security clearance to know? He's a physicist. I'm a physicist. The guy was a technician. In the Army. He took them apart and put them together a million times.'

'Those were military weapons,' said the man from Los Alamos. 'Highly sophisticated devices.'

'I'm sure the workmanship was beautiful but that has nothing to do with this,' said Chet Davis.

'I think you are oversimplifying the problem,' said the man from Los Alamos.'

'I think I'm undersimplifying it. There is a choice we have to make and it has to be made here and now. Either we accept the possibility or we don't. It's as basic as that.'

'I'm only acting in the position of a technical advisor. I don't really think I should be required to enter into the political aspects of this problem,' said the man from Los Alamos.

'Political aspects! There aren't any. We're talking about people. How would you like to be sitting on a park bench in Salt Lake City about four hours from now? How would you have liked to have been sitting on a park bench in Hiroshima?' said Chet Davis. He tossed his stick down and stood up.

'We have to tell the President,' he said to Howard Matthiessen. 'I said, we have to tell the President.'

'That's my decision, not yours,' snapped Matthiessen.

'Is it? Well I'd like to know what your decision is?' said Davis.

'This discussion is closed,' said Matthiessen.

'I'm not quite through,' said Davis. 'The President has to be informed. If you don't, I will.' The words had spilled out before he knew he was going to say them. He wanted them back. It was too late.

'Mister Davis, your usefulness to this investigation has ended,' said Matthiessen. 'Further insubordination will force me to place you in protective custody.'

'That isn't going to change anything,' said Davis.

'And neither are you,' said Matthiessen. He walked away down the hill toward the helicopter that was standing next to the crater in the street of the ghost town.

The man from Los Alamos looked at Davis and Davis

looked back. Two agents were climbing up the hill to the place where they stood. The sun was shining and the wind was kicking up a fine spray of sand.

'It's in your hands now,' said Chester Davis.

The two agents reached them. 'Nice day,' said one. 'Mister Davis?' said the other.

'What?'

'Let's go down the hill.'

Over the hubbub and confusion of many voices in general competition with each other and in specific combat for a share of the market in oats, corn, wheat and soybeans as well as for a number of other products created by nature but owned by man, the name Jake Silver was paged. He crumpled a bid he didn't want to make anyway, and tossed it on the littered floor of the Board of Trade. He went back to the telephones. It was the operator again and she told him what the problem was with his call.

'That's a car telephone number,' she said. 'We have quite a few of them out here.'

'That's nice to know. Maybe it could be fixed?' said Jake.

'Oh, that's not the problem.'

'We all got problems. What's the problem?'

'It's out of range of our transmitter, Mister Silver. We have a very powerful transmitter so it must be a long ways away,' said the operator. 'Fifty miles at least.'

'Fifty miles, a hundred and fifty miles, it's all the same to me,' said Jake Silver.

'I'm sorry, Mister Silver, but if you want to keep trying I'm sure you'll get through to the party to whom you wish to speak,' said the operator.

'Maybe you could do that for me?' said Jake Silver.

'I'm terribly sorry but we aren't allowed except for emergency purposes,' said the operator. 'This isn't an emergency, is it?'

'For me but not for you, little girlie,' said Jake. 'Thanks for letting me know.'

'My pleasure,' said the operator. 'It must be very exciting, being in the stock exchange.'

'Yeah,' said Jake. 'Very exciting.'

He hung up and drifted back into the action. The big clock that hung down from the ornate ceiling said it was 11:30am. I'll try him again at noon, like we arranged, thought Jake. Maybe the hustler who wanted his soybean oil would wait. Suddenly he realized that out there it was two hours earlier . . . that the guy must have meant 12:00 o'clock noon his time. The guy — what was his name? – he couldn't remember. Well, if he didn't reach him the deal was off. Jake shrugged. You had to be a fatalist to survive. What had the guy said his name was? Jeeves . . . ? Jorkas . . . ? Jackass . . . ? Jarhead . . . ?

Jarvis, that was it.

The freight train was moving through open country and it was moving fast trying to make up the time it had lost when it had stopped at the sidings on Spanish Fork. The grade crossings flashed by and the little towns with their abandoned stations were just a blur of water towers, backyard fences and human faces frozen in the moment of passage. The train was hauling livestock feed, some new cars, and three cattle-car loads of broken-down wild horses. The horses were packed in tight. Their noses were bruised and blistered from too much sun and too much wind. Their eyes were glazed. They simply waited.

Behind the horses was a string of tank cars. On the inside of the steel ladder that led to the top of one of them something had been taped. It wasn't easy to see but for a man who was looking it would be visible.

The helicopter taxied through a flock of commercial jet aircraft and reached the terminal building. Men jumped out and ran in a half-crouch out from under the blades toward the door and disappeared. Once inside they pushed their way through a sea of people that refused to part. Finally, they reached the street where they stood like all of the others waiting for transportation waiting for the government cars that were tied up in the traffic jam that surrounded an airport suddenly too small to cope with the sons and daughters of the Golden West who had come to Salt Lake City to celebrate Pioneer Days, to search for some meaning hidden in the past and, if possible, to take a picture of it with the expensive Japanese cameras slung around their necks.

'They got jammed up down there. It's going to be about five minutes, sir,' said one of Howard Matthiessen's aides. He had his little walkie-talkie and was speaking into it. There was nothing to do but wait. Other agents would arrive soon and face the same problem. Howard Matthiessen stood with his arms folded staring straight ahead. It was the pose of a bewildered, frightened and uncertain man. Napoleon had looked the same on his way to Elba: his world was lost, his armies defeated.

They had found Joe Morse. Some small town sheriff had reported it. They had found an empty boxcar that had been loaded with dynamite. The same sheriff had reported that, too. It was on a siding by an abandoned mine. They had found Joe Morse nailed up on a cross. He had been dead for at least two days. They had found the graves of at least ten children. Whose children they were, no one knew. It was suspected that the parents were followers of the man who had blown himself up. It was suspected that his followers were inside the church with him at the time of the explosion. No physical evidence had yet been found. It was unlikely that any would ever be found. Something else that had not been found was the plutonium. Howard Matthiessen had been assured again and again by the experts that the resources, capabilities and scientific training needed to fabricate anything resembling a bomb could not possibly be in the hands of anyone outside of the weapons establishment, certainly not a lunatic from the fundamentalist fringe. It was one thing to accept the remote possibility that a weapon existed but quite another to proceed from that raw assumption into a state of national emergency and, perhaps, even martial law imposed by a President who had been unavoidably misled by previous developments into the belief that the situation was well in hand. To tell the President now would be to admit that he, Howard Matthiessen, was totally responsible . . . totally at fault . . . totally negligent in the performance of his duties. To admit that would be to admit that everything that he stood for, believed in, had achieved in his life, was meaningless. Howard Matthiessen couldn't do it. There was only one other choice.

'Sir — ' said an agent.

'What?'

'Car's on its way in now, sir.'

'Thank you very much,' said Howard Matthiessen.

When the car pulled up he had disappeared leaving a cluster of confused agents to wait on the crowded sidewalk. The Los Alamos weapons expert was there, too. He glanced at his watch, shook his head, and took off his rimless eyeglasses. He rubbed the lenses on his sleeve, pursed his lips and studied the legs of a college girl who carried a suitcase three times too large for anyone but a pro football player. Wherever Matthiessen had gone he was in no hurry to return.

The minutes passed and the agents grew more restless. In some ways, thought the weapons scientist, they were like a herd of sheep . . . doing what they were told . . . never questioning authority . . . always polite . . . and absolutely certain in their point of view. The weapons scientist was somewhat of a student of human as well as nuclear reactions. Both subjects required a certain amount of detachment on the part of the observer. When they found Howard Matthiessen his detachment came to an abrupt end.

An agent came running with the news: 'He's in the VIP Lounge,' said the agent. 'It looks like there's been an accident.'

'What do you mean, an accident?' asked Matthiessen's personal aide.

'You know what I mean,' said the agent. 'He shot himself.'

'I don't believe it,' said the aide. 'Not Howard Matthiessen.'

'What the hell is going on,' interjected a third agent.

'Never mind what is going on. Get up to the VIP Lounge and take charge. Keep the local law enforcement out of it. Do you understand? Out of it.'

'Yes, sir,' said the agent and he was gone.

The rest of the agents huddled together, then split into twos and threes and drove away in the cars that had arrived. The weapons scientist stood watching. Finally there was only himself and Matthiessen's personal aide. 'What are you going to do?' asked the weapons scientist.

'That hasn't been decided,' said the agent.

'You know the situation. Don't you think some steps ought to be taken immediately?' said the weapons scientist.

'Which situation?' said the agent.

'The bomb situation,' said the weapons scientist.

'What bomb situation?' said the agent.

'What bomb situation?' said the weapons scientist. He was truly astounded.

'Mister Matthiessen isn't in the habit of confiding information until he feels sure that it is pertinent to Bureau activities,' said the agent. 'If there's something about a bomb how about a quick explanation of what it is.'

'It seems to me that this thing is falling apart,' said the weapons scientist. 'I'd like to talk to Chet Davis. Do you know where he is?'

'No,' said the agent. 'And I don't have any more time to waste on this. See me in the VIP Lounge.' He turned and went back inside the building leaving the man from Los Alamos surrounded by a screaming mob of Cub Scouts who were waiting to be loaded into a charter bus. The sun was out bright and hot and the wind held the American flags straight on their poles. The desert air was so dry that it rasped his throat. Somehow, through an alchemy of events which he would never understand the responsibility had been thrust into the hands of this man. It was unfair, unjust and wrong. Chet Davis had climbed out on the end of a long limb – and it had been chopped off. The same thing could happen to him. He was perfectly aware of that. He stood looking vacantly around at all of the people. None of them were sitting on park benches and all of them were strangers. But they were real people, not abstractions. He pushed his way through the glass doors into the terminal.

Twenty minutes later all of the long distance voices and the constant clicking of connections had been reduced to one final click and one last voice which was quite recognizable.

'Mister President,' said the man from Los Alamos. 'I'm afraid I have some bad news . . . ' he began.

'That's right, he was in here, oh, maybe three weeks ago. Bought a couple of remote installations and some other stuff, too,' said the man from Ten-Four Communications Systems.

'Did he say what he was going to be doing with it?' asked Eddie Shigata. 'Did he say anything at all?'

'Couldn't tell you that. It was my partner who took care of it. I'm just looking through the books here.'

'You said he bought some other things, too?'

'Well, there's a list of it here. You want me to read it out?'

'Just tell me what it was,' said Eddie.

'Let's see . . . Looks like a lot of relays and interconnects, that's about all,' said the man from Ten-Four.

'What are they used for?' said Eddie.

'Most anything you want. Turn things on, turn things off.'

'How do they work?'

'Well, suppose you've got a furnace and you want it turned on. What you do is pick up your phone and call it up.'

'Then what happens?'

'Well, the old furnace just starts right up,' said the man from Ten-Four. 'A lot of folks use it that way. Saves energy.'

'What if it was in a car?' said Eddie.

'Same thing. Don't know what there is anyone could use it for in a car but they could do it if they wanted,' said the man from Ten-Four. 'Long as it was in range.'

'What's the range?'

'Up around here, about fifty to seventy-five miles. We got the Salt Lake station and that bounces a good signal. It's all automated, too, the same as the rest of the telephones.'

'How big an antenna would you need?' asked Eddie.

'Not much. Just one of those itty-bitty little things. It's all UHF. Or you could use an FM. That works pretty well, too.'

'How many people have those kind of phones up there?' asked Eddie.

'I don't know. Might be two, three thousand of them,' said the man from Ten-Four. 'Sell them like hot cakes. That and CB.'

'What about the numbers?'

'Same as any other telephone number.'

'Is there any way I could find out what numbers he might be using on those phones?' asked Eddie.

'You'd have to talk to old Ma Bell on that,' said the man from Ten-Four. 'She's the one that knows if anyone does.'

'What do you mean by that?' asked Eddie.

'Could be an unlisted number,' said the man from Ten-Four. 'A lot of them are these days.'

Chapter Twenty

The pendulum inside the wall clock on the freight office wall had stopped with its hands on high noon, some year or other. Everybody had a digital watch these days Mulloy didn't have a watch at all. It had belonged to his father and now it belonged to the YMCA in Tucson. It was the only thing of his father's he'd ever had and now it was gone and that was just as well. Maybe the memories would leave me alone, too. But it seemed there would always be another local historian in another rotten town to remind Mulloy of who he was. At least there was that to look forward to.

The old man was flopped in the corner with his head under a newspaper and his feet up against a cold radiator. 'What time is it?' Mulloy asked him.

'Daytime.'

'Well, get up and go on out to the car and listen to the radio until you hear the time,' said Mulloy. 'Then don't forget to come back and tell me what it is.'

His bones creaked and he went outside. Mulloy went back to the teletype machine. It wasn't saying anything but pretty soon it would because that was the way things worked. Put something in and something comes back. Not true of slot machines. True of most other machines. His mind wandered. It was very tired. There was nothing I could do but wait and try not to worry about his future. Through the dirty window of the freight office I could see down the tracks leading off into the desert and beyond that to some farther nothing. It was a good thing that it was Sunday. There was no one likely to be around except maybe the Sheriff of La Vern and his friends, if he had any.

Something tapped Mulloy on his bad arm and it hurt enough to make him yell. It was Arkansas Slim's index finger. 'Don't do that!' said Mulloy.

'You ought to have it looked over,' Slim said. 'Seems to me I remember a fellow broke his arm jumping off a freight and he died of it. Took a few days before he was finished though. Seems to me that happened about 1937, maybe it was '38. It was up over near Colorado Springs. Seems to me — '

'Why don't you shut up about what it seems to you?' said Mulloy.

'I only came in to tell you that it's pretty near on to ten o'clock, that's all I came to tell you,' said Arkansas.

'Go on over there and go back to sleep,' Mulloy told him.

'I weren't asleep, I was thinking.'

'What about?'

'About getting off the rails for good,' said Arkansas. 'Seems like maybe my time has come. Things are changing.'

'Nothing's changed. It's all in your head Mulloy told him.

'I don't know about that,' said Arkansas. 'Look at you.'

'I'm just tired. There's nothing the matter with me,' said Mulloy.

'Nothing you can fix, anyways.'

'What do you mean by that?' said Mulloy.

'You never learned nothing,' said Arkansas. 'You never learned when to quit.'

'Why don't you leave me alone and shut up, too, while you're at it,' said Mulloy.

'I ain't got nothing more to say, anyway,' said Arkansas, and went back to his corner leaving Mulloy to claw and scratch at the side of the cliff that life had put him on or that he had climbed. It was the same, either way – nothing but up and nothing but down. You could also beat your head in against the smooth, hard rock. There was that choice, too.

The teletype started to clatter. The yellow paper jumped and jumped again. It went on for quite a few minutes and then it stopped. Mulloy rolled out the paper and tore it off and started to read about boxcars and night freights and routing instructions and shipping dates and delivery orders.

Ah, the poor souls without the expertise and the twenty years of sitting on their butts in a rattle trap caboose – they would have no hope of understanding the mysteries and the hidden truths of all this. It took a poor ignoramous like himself, a dumb yardbull to square the side of the hypotenuse, to see that the triangle had three sides, and there was a mad logic in it that was too simple for the advanced minds of the great white-collared, law-enforcing priesthood. And now it was too late and now, boys, all you can do is get down on your knees and pray that you can lay the blame on circumstances. After an appropriate period of mourning, of course. Always let the dust settle before the white-washing begins, isn't that right, boys? Isn't that the way it will go?

There was something out there, all right, and it was probably intended to kill a lot of people. Mulloy didn't know whether he cared about them or not. People had never done him any great favors and he didn't know if they ever did each other any great ones, either. If you looked at it, it was all a mess and it was always going to be a mess and in the long run nothing anyone did was going to change it. They said, go over the hill and you did and on the other side it was waiting for you again, and you knew it would be all along. It was waiting for you and it was you, your fellow man. Mulloy laughed. It seemed kind of funny.

'What you laughing at?' asked Arkansas.

'You name it, I'm laughing at it,' said Mulloy. 'What do you think of that?'

'I think you're going queer in the head.'

'Well, what do you think about this? We're getting in that Sheriff's car out there and we're going to get the hell out of here.'

'Moving don't interest me,' said Arkansas. 'I been moving too much.'

'You stay here and they'll pick you up. They'll put you in a jail somewhere,' said Mulloy.

'I ain't done nothing.'

'You've been with me and that's enough,' said Mulloy. 'You understand what I'm telling you?'

'Where we going?'

'Don't worry about it. I'll let you off when we get there and you can go back home. You can go back down to Mexico. I'll take you myself.'

'I don't need your help to get there.'

'Well, you need it to get out of here. Let's go,' Mulloy said. The old man hoisted himself up and they went outside into the daylight. They took the road back down out of the hills and then they were on the desert again with the sun behind them bright and strong. Ahead of them there was nothing to see but pavement and then there was the road-block – two trucks and a car about a mile ahead. Mulloy could see them but they probably couldn't see him yet through the glare. He pulled over and stopped.

'No use doing that,' said old Arkansas.

'What do you mean no use doing that?' said Mulloy.

'If you want to get around them you have to go off that-away — ' He pointed out into the sagebrush and the sand.

'What's over there?'

'Nothing for a while, but there's a road.'

'Oh, there's a road is there? How the hell do you know there's a road?' said Mulloy.

'Well, I know a few things you don't,' said Arkansas.

'How am I supposed to get over there in this?' asked Mulloy.

'It don't look that bad to me,' said Arkansas.

'How far over there?'

'Ten, fifteen miles.'

'And where is this road supposed to go?'

'Nevada,' said Arkansas. 'Ain't much of a road but they used to use it for one thing and another, mostly for running whiskey.'

'How long ago was that?'

'1932.'

So off they bounced into the desert in search of ancient history. There wasn't really anything else to do but try it.

The car bounced and yawed and picked up a load of brush which would get caught up underneath and then break

away to make room for more. There were a few bumps but
no gulleys and the ground was baked into a hard crust. None
too hard for me, thought Mulloy. They were raising up a big
cloud of dust and the wind was blowing it high. After a
couple of miles he stopped and took a look back. There were
two more clouds of dust and they were coming his way.
Four-wheel drive trucks, no doubt, the kind that sit way up
high on their wheels with a Redneck and a rack full of guns
on top.

Mulloy drove on and they came following: the cats and
the mouse. There was an unsubtle change in the country: it
got rougher. Plenty of rocks and sand and nasty little craters
that made the junk heap of a car lurch and dive and then
smash back down on its worn out shocks. Every time it
happened fire shot through the broken arm. The pain helped
to keep Mulloy awake.

They crossed a salt pan and when they reached the other
side the pursuing dust clouds were not too far behind. The
ground rose gently toward a line of hills. There was a cactus
forest in between and Mulloy tried dodging his way through.
He hit one with the front fender and there was the crunch of
collapsing metal. Green juice squirted all over the windshield. He turned on the wipers but only one of them worked.
If they didn't make it soon, they weren't going to make it at
all.

Mulloy wanted to know what time it was. He told the old
man to turn on the radio. Arkansas couldn't find a station
and then he found one. It was some oily-voiced phony calling himself the Reverend Peabody telling people to be sure
and tune in on his all-night talk-show. And then there was a
commercial and then the announcer said, 'And now it's time
for Paul Harvey.' So they had to listen to Paul Harvey. The
ground got rocky and bumpy and Mulloy had to put the car
into low gear. They crawled up a pretty steep hill with the
wheels spinning out a shower of stones. Going down the
other side it was even steeper. They hit a big rock and
the muffler fell off. The radio said: 'And now the time is
10:55am.'

At the bottom of the hill was the road. Mulloy got the car over a ditch somehow and they were on it. As roads go, it wasn't much. Mulloy had the feeling it was going to get even worse. The ruts headed up into the hills and they followed them. In the mirror he could see the pickup trucks about a quarter of a mile behind him.

The Sheriff of La Vern had his sawed-off shotgun locked up in its rack between the seats. The key was probably on the keyring in the ignition switch. Mulloy tried to explain it to the old man. The old man tried to understand but he shut off the engine two or three times anyway before he got the other keys clear. Then he started to fumble around with the lock. By that time they were up in the hills winding around and around trying to dodge the rock slides and not go off the road over the drop off on the other side. They reached the top still in one piece and started down. Mulloy began to believe that it wasn't all that hopeless. Then he saw the bridge. It was way down at the bottom of the ravine and he could see where parts of it were starting to fall in.

'Why didn't you tell me about that?' said Mulloy.

'Because I forgot it,' said Arkansas.

'Oh, you forgot it,' said Mulloy. 'You forgot it.'

'Anyway, there ain't no water,' said the old man.

'That's right, there ain't no water,' said Mulloy.

'Well — ' said Slim above the backfiring of the engine.

'Ah, shut up. Just shut up,' said Mulloy. The old man gave him a mournful look and Mulloy ignored him.

They went down and down and then they were there: The so-called bridge was a hundred yards ahead of them and the trucks were coming about a hundred yards behind. There was nothing to do but try it so Mulloy tried it. He gave it the gun and pointed the nose of the car at what was left of the wooden bridge. They hit at fifty miles an hour and shot out into space. It seemed like a long time before they hit the other side of the ravine and the impact blew a front tire. The car went into a skid but stayed in one piece. They continued at a crawl for a couple of hundred yards. Then Mulloy stopped and looked back. The bridge had collapsed and the trucks were stuck on the far side. Mulloy and Slim had made it. The trucks had not.

Mulloy went another fifty yards on the wheel hub and stopped. 'Get the trunk open and get the spare,' he said. 'And get the jack, too.'

'What if they start in shooting?' said the old man.

'They won't start shooting. They're out of range,' said Mulloy. To show him he was right, he got out – and he was right.

Inside the trunk there was a bald spare and a rusty old jack. Mulloy helped him set it up and he did the work. It was taking longer than it should have but there was nothing he could do but coax him along. The last tire he'd probably changed was on a Model-T. When they were done they put the jack back in the trunk and closed it up. Mulloy told him to get in and started to do it himself. Slim stood there for a minute and Mulloy thought he was being proud of himself. Just to show the world that he counted for something, too, he stuck up his arm and shook his fist at the men standing down by the bridge. One of them raised up his gun and took the kind of long shot that makes deer hunters laugh at each other. The bullet hit him smack in the chest. He went down. The sound caught up. It boomed back and forth off of the hills. Then it was quiet again and Slim lay there in his own blood and his wreckage and there was nothing anyone could do. The bullet had delivered the message, which was full of the sad insanity of us all.

Mulloy dragged him around to the side of the car and tumbled him into the back seat. He weighed about as much as a dead bird, the kind that people toss in their garbage cans and forget about.

'If you'd just done what I told you to do, they wouldn't have shot you,' he said. 'You dumb old son of a bitch, what's the matter with you?'

But he had nothing more to say.

Mulloy got the car started and drove it up the other side of the mountain until the bridge was a tiny little thing down at the bottom of the canyon and then it was gone.

He had nothing more to say but Mulloy kept talking to him all of the way down out of the hills and back into the desert again. None of what he said made much sense and none of it mattered. Not even when he told him he was sorry.

The road went on and on through the wasteland. The car left various pieces of itself strewn in its wake. For some reason the engine wouldn't give up. The sky was gray and saturated with wind-blown dust. In the distance there was a flash of movement: cars and trucks. The road took me there. It was the Interstate Highway. He got on it through a big hole in the cyclone wire fence that someone had crashed a car through.

He got on the tail of a high balling truck but he pulled steadily away. The sheriff's automobile was not doing too well. There was a road sign ahead. NORTH LAS VEGAS, it said. 25.

He fooled with the radio and got a station. It told him the time. It was two minutes to noon. The freight he was looking for, the freight from Salt Lake City was due at 12:14.

'Keep trying,' said Chet Davis. 'Keep trying.'

'I'm sorry, sir, but all of the lines are still busy,' said the Chicago operator. 'If you would like to place the call at a later time—'

'This is an emergency. Can't you cut through?'

'I'm not allowed to do that without authorization, sir,' said the operator. 'Is this a medical emergency?'

'Yes,' said Chet Davis. 'You could call it that.'

'Well, I'll try,' said the operator. 'And your name?'

'Doctor Davis.'

'Well, I'll try, Doctor,' said the operator and the line went silent leaving Chet Davis to look at his watch and at the group of men who clustered around the sheet-covered body of Howard Matthiessen which lay on the stretcher that the airport medical service had wheeled into the VIP lounge. His death had delivered the final blow to what little control of events now remained. The FBI had become a headless chicken that fluttered wildly trying to reconnect severed nerves to mindless sinews.

'You're number is ringing now, sir,' said the operator.

'Chicago Commodities Exchange,' said the voice at the other end.

'Is there a Jake Silver there?' said Chet Davis.

'You mean the broker?'

'That's right. Can you get him on this line?'

'Hold on,' said the voice. Chet waited. 'Sorry,' said the voice, 'he's left for the day.'

'Thanks,' said Chet Davis. 'Thanks a lot.' He hung up. The brink had been reached and now everything was toppling over it. 'Is there any other number that I can reach for you?' asked the operator.

'Try this one,' said Chet Davis. It was Eddie Shigata's number. Eddie might as well know. Everyone had a right to know.

Chet Davis' voice was flat and emotionless. He said, 'It's a phone number. The thing is rigged to a phone call and it's coming from Chicago.'

'That's what I thought,' said Eddie Shigata.

They tracked it down up in Ogden. It's some guy who sells commodities. The son of a bitch got ahold of one of his tank cars, drained it out and used it for the bomb. Soybean oil. It's all over the ground up at some siding where he put it all together. He was one crazy clever son of a bitch,' said Chet Davis.

'But they aren't letting it get into Salt Lake City,' said Eddie. 'They've stopped all the incoming railroad traffic, haven't they?'

'It's not coming to Salt Lake,' said Chet Davis. 'It never was supposed to. It's in Las Vegas. It wasn't your fault, Eddie. Just remember that.'

'It was my fault,' said Eddie. 'I told you and you listened. It was my fault.'

'There wasn't enough time, Eddie,' said Chet Davis.
There was silence between them.

'When?' asked Eddie.

'Anytime, I think,' said Chet Davis. 'He was set up to make the call. He doesn't know.'

'I'm going to the railroad yard,' said Eddie.

'Sure,' said Chet. 'I hope you make it.'

'Any chance of evacuating the city?' said Eddie.

'No time left. It would just start a panic,' said Chet Davis. 'People indoors have a better chance.'

'I'm going to the railroad yard,' said Eddie Shigata.

'I'm sorry, Eddie,' said Chet Davis. But the telephone line was already dead.

Half of Las Vegas was still sleeping off the night before and the other half was staying inside, out of the wind that was stiffening the flags out in front of the hotels, the gambling palaces and the office buildings. Mulloy had the sheriff's siren turned on full-blast and the red lights flashing. He almost hit a kid and his dog and then he almost hit an armored car that was turning out of a hidden driveway that probably led straight to a Swiss Bank Account. There was the smell of burning motor oil and the sound of a connecting rod knocking itself to pieces. About three long blocks from the Railroad Yard the engine blew itself to pieces. He got out and started to run. Then he stopped and ran back. He took the sheriff's shotgun and started to run again.

When Mulloy reached the main gate of the yard, he waved it at the security guard. He took one look and took off. Nobody likes to see a shotgun. The control tower was in the middle of all the tracks. He went up the steps and slipped and cut his jaw. He got up and made it to the top. The man inside took one look and started to put up his hands. 'Now, just calm down. Nobody's going to hurt you,' he said, edging toward the door.

'The twelve o'clock freight from Salt Lake City,' said Mulloy. 'Where is it?'

'Now you just keep calm,' the guard repeated. 'Nobody wants to hurt you, Mister.'

'Tell me where it is or I'll blow off your head,' said Mulloy.

'It's there,' said the guard. 'It's right down there. They're breaking it up. Don't blow off my head. I didn't do anything to you.'

Mulloy looked down and there they were.

'Get a switch engine on that last string of cars,' he said. 'Those tank cars, do you see the ones I mean?'

'I see them. If that's what you want, I'll do it. You just let me do it and I'll do it,' the guard said picking up one of the phones. 'Get a yard engine on that string of tank cars and do it fast,' he said into the receiver.

'OK, that's good,' said Mulloy. 'Now what you're going to do is give me a clear run out of here on the line to Yucca Flat.'

'That's a government line.'

'Just do like I tell you and maybe you'll live long enough to be a hero,' said Mulloy. 'Otherwise, I can pretty much guarantee you'll be dead, I'll be dead and a lot of other people, too.'

'You're the boss.' He went to the board and started to press buttons. Red lights changed to green lights and numbers appeared on the little television screens. 'OK, it's all set,' the guard told Mulloy. 'You see that. They've got her all hooked up down there. There's nothing for you to worry about.'

'Well, here's something for you to worry about,' said Mulloy. 'There's a bomb in one of those tankers down there and if you want it to go off and erase half this city you just start playing with those switches after I pull out of here.'

The guard stared at him and said nothing.

'If anyone wants to know, tell them that it was Mulloy. Just tell them that.'

He went down the steps. There were a couple of men standing by the switch engine. He waved the shot gun and they backed off. He climbed up into the cab and started it rolling. There were ten tank cars behind him and behind them three cattle cars full of tired out old horses. It was too late to do anything about the man who he saw climbing up the side of the last one. He was going for the ride, too. He was some idiot who didn't know how it was going to end. By the time they cleared the last of the switches and sidings he was on top and working his way forward. It wasn't easy at fifty miles an hour. Mulloy could see his black hair blowing in the breeze and damned if he wasn't a Jap. There was nothing left to do now but to sit with his foot on the dead man's throttle and watch the suburbs fly by and to look at the swimming pools in the big backyards. It was seventy-five miles into the proving grounds. He had a feeling that this freight train wasn't going to make it that far.

'What I'm saying is this,' said Marty Shapiro's head sticking up out of the steam box which was across from Jake Silver, whose head was doing likewise. 'I'm saying that eighty per-cent of the people in this country are a bunch of dumb slobs. Tell them what they want to hear and you'll make them happy.'

Jake Silver didn't agree. He chomped down hard on his cigar and looked at Marty's glistening bald head. 'So maybe we're dumb slobs, too,' he said. 'Let's talk about something else.'

'What else is there?' said Marty. 'The world is falling to pieces.'

'Maybe so,' said Jake. 'Maybe so.'

An attendant shuffled through the big, marble-floored room where the lines of steam boxes squatted each with its occupant.

'Bring me a phone,' said Jake Silver. 'I got to make a call.'

The telephone appeared and it was plugged into a wall outlet. The attendant stood waiting. 'Never mind, I'll dial it myself,' said Jake. The lid on the box flew open, he stood up and stepped out. The attendant presented him with a towel and draped it around his paunch. Jake started to dial. The deal with the hustler was already lost but he didn't want to lose what he had. By now, the guy with the car telephone should be somewhere within range of something, thought Jake. He had reached the next to last digit when the door of the steam room burst open and as Jake watched in astonishment two men sprinted across the floor toward him. One of them slipped and fell down. The other one tore the phone out of Jake's hands and pulled the cord out of the wall socket. The man who had fallen down picked himself up. The man who had grabbed the telephone held it in both hands; both of them looked at Jake Silver who shrugged and shook his head.

Eddie could see it. Reaching it was another problem. Looking forward he crouched on top of the cattle car that was full of horses and shielded his eyes against the onrushing wind. The antenna that led to the bomb was on the third tank car forward. It was taped to the ladder. The wind had torn it loose and it flapped wildly back and forth. To get to it he would have to cross the gaps between two cars that lurched, swayed and shuddered over a blurred abyss of railroad track. If the man inside the cab of the diesel would only stop the train, the problem was solved. Eddie had waved, Eddie had shouted, his voice lost in the wind, and finally he had accepted the fact that the man was paying no attention, whoever he was, to Eddie Shigata. A minute or two earlier and he could have reached him before the train left the railroad yard. Could have explained. Now there was nothing he could do but try to reach it in his way. Holding on to the slats of the cattle car, he swung over the edge searching for a foothold, found one, then another. He worked his way down until he was standing on the solid steel of the coupling. He rested. Out of the corner of his eye he saw that the desert had risen suddenly to reshape itself into arid and desolate hills. The train was slowing down. It was starting to climb a steep grade. Eddie turned. He braced himself and got ready to jump for the ladder on the last tank car.

At the Las Vegas telephone exchange, Helen West was getting ready to go to lunch. She was going to meet a couple of her friends who worked in the business office upstairs and they were planning to spend the hour at a department store. They did it two or three times a week. So did all the other operators in the Long Distance section.

It had been a busy morning. A lot of people were trying to make hotel reservations and then there was that man from Chicago, that Mister Silver at the Stock Exchange who was trying to reach the man with the car telephone. He had sounded very upset when the call had failed to go through. It was probably an important deal, thought Helen West. Not knowing exactly why she was doing it but with a feeling of curiosity and a glow of good will she decided to try the number herself. A picture of Mister Silver had formed in her head. He was a kindly, silver-haired gentleman who rode in the back of a chauffeur-driven limousine to and from a fabulous house in the country.

Her mind full of these thoughts, she started to punch the buttons.

At the top of the long grade the tracks ran level for a quarter of a mile toward a wall of solid rock. The entrance to the tunnel was at the base of a two thousand foot cliff.

The locomotive and the thirteen cars that it had brought up from the desert far below now appeared. Moving slowly but steadily gathering speed, the train headed toward the mouth of the tunnel. Two hundred yards from the concrete abutment that surrounded the entrance a man appeared on the bottom of the steps that led up to the cab of the locomotive. He paused and looked forward and then to the rear at the man who was clinging to the side of a tank car. He waved one of his arms in a gesture of terrible finality and yelled something that was forever lost in the roar of the diesel, the rumble of steel turning against steel. Forty yards from the mouth of the tunnel, the man on the steps jumped. His body rolled over and over and down a drainage slope. The locomotive disappeared into the mountain and the rest of the train followed. And then there was silence.

Then the pine trees shook and the mountain trembled and then the whole world seemed to fling itself toward the sky in a series of spasms and contractions that would shake the seismographs. Then the shaking stopped, it was quiet again. A pall of dust hung over the mountain.

Deep within burned a fire that no one could ever quench. It would burn silently, in an eternal flame of nucleii bathed in the soft, fierce glow of atomic radiation, walled off from the world like a distant, tiny star.

Through the haze that lingered over the railroad tracks, a man appeared. He was covered with dirt, dust and blood. He limped away from the collapsed mouth of the railroad tunnel. It was Mulloy.

Chapter Twenty-one

The Greyhound bus stopped on the main highway and let Mulloy off. The people inside looked at him through the tinted windows and then the bus pulled away. He started to walk down the road that led into town. He had a newspaper rolled up under his good arm. The other one was sticking straight out, all wired up and in a plaster cast. It made him feel like one of the tin hockey goalies that you paid a quarter to operate in the penny arcade. He was wearing a pair of baggy blue trousers and a grey, jailhouse shirt that still smelled of sweat and old mothballs.

'That arm won't ever be much good and it's your own fault for not getting it taken care of,' the bright young doctor had said. He had spent two days answering a lot of stupid questions and then they wanted him to sign the papers that said: In the interests of national security I agree to keep my mouth shut. And he did. Then they let him loose. Some kind soul gave him ten dollars for a bus ticket and told him to get out of Las Vegas and stay out. The fare to Pearl's place was $9.85.

He walked up the middle of the empty street and there it was. Someone had smashed in the fancy front door and ripped up the fake gingerbread awning. He went inside where everything was in a worse mess. The bartender was nursing a bottle of whiskey and one of the girls was coming down the grand staircase dragging a big blue suitcase. She was abandoning the good ship lollipop. He asked the man behind the bar where Pearl was hiding out. His eyes flicked in the direction of the stairs but his expression remained the same.

She was upstairs lying on the brass bed in the big room with the mirrors. They were all smashed and shattered and the sunlight that came streaming through the cathedral windows covered her with a tapestry of broken images. She had a black eye and a puffed-up lip. Their eyes met and then slipped away from each other again like two strange old dogs in search of something better.

'It was my fault,' said Mulloy. 'I'm sorry. I know that's not what you want to hear but that's all I can say. If you hadn't come over there and done what you did it wouldn't have happened. Where the hell was the sheriff of this town?'

'With *him*,' she said.

'I guess I'm just always going to be the way I am,' said Mulloy. 'I can't seem to help it, Pearl.'

'No,' she said. 'You can't.'

'Well, that's the way it is,' said Mulloy.

She didn't say anything. He sat down on the corner of the bed. It squeaked softly. The canary in the overturned cage in the corner of the room answered the sound with a little song.

'Would you go to San Francisco with me?' said Mulloy. 'We could talk a few things over. We could do that.'

She didn't say yes but she didn't say no.